I0629526

LITTLE JAR OF TEETH

DARK STORIES TO KEEP YOU UP AT NIGHT

A. L. HATCHER

Little Jar of Teeth: Dark Stories to Keep You Up At Night Copyright © 2024 by A.L. Hatcher

Published in the United States by A.L. Hatcher, Author

All rights reserved.

No portion of this book may be reproduced, distributed, or transmitted in any form or by any means, including photocopying, recording, or other electronic or mechanical methods, without prior written permission from the author, except as permitted by U.S. copyright law. For permission requests, contact the author at alhatcherauthor@gmail.com.

The stores, names, characters, organizations, and incidents portrayed in this production are either the product of the author's imagination or are used fictitiously.

ISBN: 979-8-9889438-4-6

ePUB ISBN: 979-8-9889438-5-3

Cover design by C. Rothe

PRAISE FOR A.L. HATCHER

Praise for The Blood Eagle

"From the first chapter, I was absolutely hooked. Fast paced, engaging, twisty, and downright horrifying (in all the best possible ways)." — Alex, Amazon review

"... the crime scenes were very realistic.... I might or might not have looked behind me often last night after reading some of the murder scenes!" —Kiara Yaeger, author of *Annoy Me More* and *Back Home at Shawnee Creek*

Praise for River of Lies

"...if you're searching for a book that will consume you, captivate you, and leave you breathless with anticipation, look no further than *River of Lies*." —Robin G-V, Amazon review

"Put your seat belt on and hang on for this one! I can't recommend this book enough!!"—Heather, Goodreads

"Tess is back and with a vengeance, proving she's one tough cookie... and a smart one at that, when she picks up a missing person case that has several twists and turns. Fun read!"—J.C. Fuller, author of *Black Bear Alibi* and *The Push*

Also by A.L. Hatcher

The Tess Dane Thrillers:

The Blood Eagle (book 1)

River of Lies (book 2)

For Chelsea and Pat
Thank you for all of your excitement and feedback
for all of these stories and more. You mean more to me
than you know.

And to all readers who like to read shorter, messed-up
stories but don't have the time to commit to a full-length
book. This one's for you.

TRIGGER WARNINGS

This book is full of dark and creepy stories. Some are worse than others. Please read the list of trigger warnings below and decide if this book is for you. If the trigger warnings are limited to just one story, the title of the story is listed. Otherwise, they are found throughout the book. Please read responsibly.

*Murder—including being axed to death—You can't write a creepy story without someone taking a dirt nap!
*Domestic violence (*The Blizzard, The Bloody Benders*)
*Being buried alive (*The Bells of St. Andrews Cemetery*)
*Animal attacks
*Mention of animal death (*The Animal Within*)
*Mention of abuse of an animal corpse (*The Animal Within*)
*Mention of drug abuse/use (*The Animal Within)*
*Having your teeth removed from your skull... while

you're still alive. (*Little Jar of Teeth*)

*True-life serial killer families (*The Bloody Benders*)

*Some language throughout

*Descriptions of dead bodies—including dismemberment

*A plane crash (*The Alaskan Terror*)

*Some mild sexual innuendos (*The Bloody Benders*)

CONTENTS

1

— • —

Sweet Caroline

"Do you know where your daughter is?" the male voice whispered harshly through my phone's speaker. It was sometime after midnight and my groggy brain was still half asleep. Shaking my head in confusion, I tried to process what the caller had said.

"What? Who is this?" I asked, rolling over awkwardly in bed, trying not to wake my husband next to me. Except...he wasn't there. *What is going on?* My half-asleep brain wondered.

"It's a simple question. Do you know where your daughter is?" the caller asked again. This time, the hair on the back of my neck stood on end. Who was this, calling me in the middle of the night? And where was Paul? He wasn't in bed with me.

I quickly pulled the duvet back, and slid my legs out of bed, while fumbling around to turn the bedside lamp on.

"Of course, I know where my daughter is. Who is this?" I snapped with much more bravado than I felt. Caroline was tucked in bed across the hall, her sister Ava in the neighboring room.

I was met with silence. Pulling the cell phone away from my face I noted that the call was still connected. We were at two minutes, thirteen seconds, and counting. The caller ID read 'Unknown.'

"Look mister, I don't know what kind of sick joke you're playing, but leave me the hell alone," I growled and hung up the phone.

I had a meeting for work first thing in the morning and a whole laundry list of things to get done. I needed all the sleep I could get. Annoyed at the crank call, and at my husband for most likely falling asleep again in the chair in the living room, I grumpily plopped back down on the bed to go back to sleep.

Except the mom in me couldn't do it.

No... Now that the seed of doubt had been planted in my mind that Caroline or Ava might not *actually* be in their beds, it was growing out of control. Tendrils of "what ifs" and leaves of "if only you'd checked" began growing, causing my anxiety to spike and my imagination to run wild.

Throwing back the covers for the second time in as many minutes, I flipped on the bedside lamp again with a sigh of frustrated resignation and quietly padded over to the bedroom door. Opening it, I peered out into the darkened hallway.

The soft glow from the TV in the living room cast an eerie moving light across the family pictures hanging on the walls. I strained my ears, listening for the TV, but heard nothing. *Paul must have it muted*, I thought to myself.

Walking down the hall, I quietly opened Ava's door and peered inside her room. Her nightlight cast an array of constellations slowly moving across the ceiling and pale pink walls. From the doorway, I could see Ava's small face; her eyes closed, the fisted blanket pulled up under her chin.

Banjo, our forty-pound mutt, lifted his head from where he'd been sleeping on the foot of Ava's bed. His black and white tail immediately began thumping when he saw me spying on Ava.

"It's alright," I whispered as I quietly crept further into the room to check the window latches. Locked as usual. Turning toward the bed, I watched my daughter sleep quietly for a second, her breathing slow and even. *Everything's fine*, I told myself. I patted Banjo's soft head on the way out of the room, leaving the door slightly ajar for the dog to escape if he wanted.

Stepping out into the hallway, I glanced toward the living room, wondering again where Paul was. I decided to check on Caroline first and then seek out my wayward husband. Pausing in front of Caroline's door, I turned the knob and opened the door.

The room was dark except for a small string of fairy lights that Caroline had hung from her windows. The warm glow gave the small bedroom a cozy feel, especially when she was reading one of her many books in her nest chair.

It was a Friday night, so I was kind of surprised that I didn't find her nestled in the chair with a book and a bag of Doritos. Always an introvert, she had a small circle of close friends, but they rarely met up outside of school. If Caroline ever did go out on the weekends, she always told her father and me where she was going. As long as she was back by curfew, we rarely said anything. We just wanted to know where she was in case of an emergency.

I glanced at her bed but found it empty, the blankets still pulled up in a haphazard effort to make the bed. Where was she? Suddenly I started to panic, but then the rational part of my brain kicked in. *Relax... maybe she's watching TV with Paul? Maybe she's in the shower? Maybe she de-*

cided to go out after all and told Paul–I knew how well he
communicates...

Casting a glance around the small bedroom for any sign of where she might have gone, I went to find Paul in the living room.

An episode of Friends played muted on the TV as I entered the living room. Paul, as predicted, sat reclined in his usual chair, mouth agape, remote in his hand.

Caroline wasn't there.

"Paul," I nudged him but got no response. "Paul," I repeated, this time with more panic and annoyance in my voice. It did the trick.

"What?" he asked, wiping at his chin as he quickly sat up straighter as though he hadn't just been snoring to high heaven.

"Where's Caroline?" I asked without preamble. Not waiting for his pupils to catch up, I flipped on the lamp next to him and he let out a hiss.

"What are you talking about?" he whined, holding his hand up over his eyes. "What's going on?"

"Where is Caroline?" I repeated, staring him down, my anxiety spiking like needles all over my skin.

"How should I know?" Paul huffed at me, annoyed I'd woke him. "In bed, like normal? God, Heather, turn the light off." He leaned back in his seat again and acted like he was about to close his eyes again, too tired to talk to me.

"Paul!" I snapped, reaching for his shoulders and giving them a gentle shake. His sleepy eyes opened again and slowly focused on me.

"I just got a phone call. Some creepy guy asked if I knew where my daughter was. I thought he was full of crap and hung up on him," I explained slowly, making sure he kept looking at me, following along. "Then I decided to check on the girls. Caroline isn't in her room."

"What?" Paul asked incredulously, appearing fully awake now. He stood up then and I watched as he quickly made his way down the hall to Caroline's room. I followed.

He flipped on the light and I found him standing in the middle of the room, slowly turning around in a circle, a look of desperation etched into his face. Sensing I was there, he looked over at me. "Where is she?"

"I don't know," I shrugged, trying to tramp down the anxiety. "I was hoping you knew." I felt like vomiting as I watched him shake his head. "I'm going to finish checking the house. Maybe she's just getting a shower?"

"I'll see if her car is here," he offered, already moving past me. The obvious thing to check, of course. She'd just turned sixteen a few months ago and Paul had gifted her an old 2005 Honda Civic with a ton of miles on it and no air conditioner. You'd thought he'd given her a Porsche by the squeal she'd let out when he'd produced the keys.

Swallowing the bile that rose when I found the bathroom empty, I quickly headed for the kitchen, pausing by the laundry room on the way. No Caroline. Where was she?

I met Paul coming in the back door, a grim look on his face. A slight shake of his head told me her car was missing.

"We need to call the police," my voice came out more like a screech of terror than a well-formed thought. Paul just stood there, running his hands through his hair, a look of utter bewilderment on his face. Annoyed at his sudden inactivity, I ran back to our bedroom to grab my cell phone. We'd long ago gotten rid of our landline, and at that moment, I wished we still had a phone in every room.

Just as I approached the bed, looking around for my phone, I heard it begin to ring. *Maybe it was Caroline?* Frantically grabbing at the blankets, I flipped them over, searching for the phone. My anxiety spiked, worried that the call would disconnect before I found the phone.

Giving the duvet a final shake, I sighed in relief when I felt the weight of the phone fall to the floor. Stooping low, I grabbed it and pressed the green answer button, barely registering the fact that the screen read 'Unknown' again.

"Hello?" I breathed, hoping, wishing, it was my sweet daughter's voice I would hear. My hopes were short-lived when I heard a deep raspy laugh coming through the speaker.

"Hello, Heather. Have you found sweet Caroline yet?" came the voice of the man who'd called moments ago and shattered our world.

"Who is this?" I demanded, anger and fear instantly rising in me. I wanted to reach through the phone and choke the life out of him until he told me where my daughter was.

"Now where's the fun in that?" he purred in my ear. "Tsk, tsk."

"Where is my daughter, you sick fuck?" I demanded again, surprised at my profanity. Usually, I was one to find alternatives for such words, but I was not in that mindset now. "Where is Caroline? Tell me now or I'll call the police." It was an idle threat. I fully intended to call the police regardless of whether he told me where Caroline was.

"Tell you what..." the man offered, his voice deep and somewhat familiar, yet woefully foreign to me. "Let's play a game. Rule number one: no police."

"And if I say no?" I countered, dropping to the edge of the bed with a defeated huff. Paul stood in the doorway listening to my side of the conversation, a look of confusion on his face. I pressed the 'speaker' button to include him.

"Then Caroline dies," the man stated bluntly as though he were reporting the weather or hog belly prices on the daily news. I closed my eyes, squeezing my lips in a grim line, willing myself not to cry out. I jolted when the bed shifted under me, but when I opened my eyes, I realized that it was just Paul, looking as desperate as I felt.

"Fine. We'll play. What do you want? Money?" I asked, my eyes finding Paul's in the dim light from the lamp.

A low and raspy laugh flowed from the phone's speaker. "No, I don't want your money. You'll figure it out soon enough." There was some kind of background noise. *Traffic? Was that a car door?* Everything was garbled and hard to decipher.

"So if you don't want money, then what do you want?" Paul asked, seeming to suddenly come out of his fugue.

"There's a key in your pantry. Find it. Take it to Grigby Station. Inside locker 462, you'll find your next instructions. You have one hour." The line went dead.

I turned to Paul who sat there staring numbly at the phone. "Paul, call your Mom. Ask her to come and watch Ava." I was already halfway to the hallway. Casting a glance over my shoulder, my anger surged. "Paul!"

He jumped then, turning to me before hopping up to follow me. "Call your mother!" I snapped. "Get her over here. Don't tell her anything she doesn't need to know. I'm looking for the key."

Hoping he was following through with his task, I made my way to the pantry. Yanking open the door, I did a quick visual scan of the shelves but saw nothing obvious. Shoving random cans of vegetables and soups aside, I came up empty-handed. Each move I made felt like it took moments, hours, to perform. I was stressed enough; the ticking clock didn't help me at all.

Anxiety pricked my skin, like a million tiny needles. Where was the key? I felt like the clock was ticking faster than my heart rate. I could hear Paul in the bedroom, speaking in hushed tones. Hopefully, his mother would come over to stay with Ava without asking too many questions. Fat chance.

Since the key hadn't presented itself easily, I began grabbing various canisters of dry goods and upending them in a fevered search. Flour, spaghetti noodles, quinoa, sugar, elbow macaroni, cornmeal–nothing was safe from my search. Yes, I knew I was making a huge mess. Yes, I knew I was wasting a ton of food. But at that moment, it was the least of my worries. I just wanted— no, needed— my daughter back home, safe and sound.

I'd opened all of the canisters and had found nothing. Pulling out all the storage baskets and dumping them for a quick search before moving on, had produced no key.

A frustrated cry built in my chest, my breathing becoming ragged. I told myself that I couldn't start crying. If I started now, I knew I wouldn't stop. Besides, crying would do nothing to help Caroline.

Just then, Paul entered the kitchen, his cell phone in hand. "Mom will be here in a couple of minutes," he stated, quickly surveying the mess I'd made. "Any luck?" I shook my head, my face full of sorrow.

"No, I'm still look—" It was then that I saw it. The key, just a piece of metal and orange plastic was barely visible. "There!" I gasped, reaching up to the top shelf where a jar of homemade pickles sat. My mother-in-law and I had tried our hand at pickle-making the year prior and we still had a few jars of dills left.

Grabbing the jar, I headed for the counter and tried removing the lid. It wouldn't budge. In my haste to find my daughter, to secure her safely, I didn't even think to ask Paul to open the jar. I simply checked to make sure the strainer was in the sink drain before raising the jar over my head and then throwing it with force into the sink. It shattered on impact, shards of glass and dill pickle slices covering the basin. I barely noticed the sound of the pickle juice swirling down the drain as I was already pushing pickled cucumbers out of my way to grab the orange-handled locker key.

"Ouch!" I hissed, watching as a bright red drop of blood instantly beaded up on my skin from where a shard of glass had just sliced through it. Sticking my finger in my mouth on instinct, I tasted the familiar flavors of dill and iron.

Suddenly, there was a knock at the front door, and then a voice softly calling, "Paul?"

I stuck my head around the corner, relieved to see Gina, Paul's mother, coming through my front door. For once it paid off to have my in-laws living right next door.

"In here Gina," I called quietly, trying not to wake Ava in the process. I was anxious enough dealing with *my* questions and emotions. I didn't feel like I could deal adequately with Ava's also. Besides, we were in a time crunch to get across town to Grigby Station.

Gina walked in, hair disheveled from sleep, wearing plaid pajama pants, a sweatshirt, and a robe. She'd left her shoes by the front door. The look on her face told me she had a million questions, but the look on mine must have told her that now was not a good time.

"Go. Do whatever it is you need to do. I'll keep an eye on Ava," she promised, for once seeming to understand that something unfortunate was happening, something she couldn't control. I gave her what I hoped was an appreciative look, then nodded for Paul. We quickly slid on our coats, making sure our cell phones were in our pockets. I kept the locker key grasped tightly in my fist the entire time as I slid on my tennis shoes, quietly thankful that I'd decided to wear socks and yoga pants to bed that night.

I was barely buckled in as Paul pulled out of the driveway and away from our house. I could see Gina watching us leave from where she stood in the living room peering out the front window. I felt horrible for leaving her so abruptly, but we didn't have enough time to explain it all, to answer what would no doubt be an endless list of questions.

***

Thirty-eight minutes and ten red lights later, we finally arrived at Grigby Station. The city was surprisingly busy so late at night and I felt like screaming for people to get out of our way.

Finding a parking spot near the entrance to Grigby, Paul slid the car into 'park'. I was out of the vehicle before he'd even turned it off. I heard him slam his door behind me as I ran across the wet pavement toward the train station entrance. A light mist had begun to fall, adding to the rain from earlier in the day, making everything wet. Thankful for my hoodie and yoga pants, I climbed the stairs and pulled open the glass door, Paul hot on my heels.

Inside, the terminal seemed practically deserted. A man wearing dirty, worn clothing sat in the corner on a bench, talking to himself. Up ahead of me, I could see a janitor pulling a mop bucket out of what I'm guessing was a restroom. The tires had caught on the threshold causing the dirty water to slosh everywhere. The janitor muttered to himself and began idly mopping up the mess.

Glancing around for the lockers, I saw none. Paul let out a sigh as he too, searched for them. He looked at his watch and the expression on his face told me we were running out of time.

"Where are they?" he hissed under his breath as he continued to look around. "Excuse me!" he called out to the janitor. When the old man looked in our direction, Paul began running towards him. "Where are the lockers?"

"Down that hallway. Over there," the janitor pointed down a dimly lit corridor. The light overhead flickered ominously like they do in horror movies two seconds before the monsters jumps out and eat the character's face.

That did not bode well.

We didn't have time to worry about the theatrics of it all though. Our daughter was missing and the clock was ticking. Not waiting to see if Paul followed, I quickly headed towards the dark hallway, searching for locker 462.

"Shit," Paul muttered behind me as I watched the numbers go up on the old, metal lockers. The chipped yellow paint covering the lockers was distracting as it was covered in graffiti and scratches.

"What?" I asked, not even bothering to pull my eyes away from the locker numbers. Most of the numbers were so scratched they were difficult to read and I was afraid of missing 462.

"We only have one minute left," Paul brushed past me to quickly search the numbers. I felt my pulse skyrocket in my chest again. One minute? Until the madman killed her? What stopped the clock? Us finding the locker? Or doing some sick task found within?

Tears threatened to fall again but still, I pressed on. Suddenly, Paul dropped to his knees and announced, "Here! Hand me the key." I quickly handed him the key and watched in silent horror as he turned it. The lock mechanism sounded loud, the hinges even louder, as he opened the small rectangular box.

Inside sat a manila envelope, battered and torn at the top. Paul and I looked at each other in confusion. Just as he was reaching inside, my phone began ringing, causing me to jump. Fishing it out of my pocket, I noticed the

'Unknown' on the display and my heart plummeted. I answered it and immediately put it on speaker so that Paul could hear.

"Let me talk to Caroline," I snapped into the receiver, bypassing all preamble. I was rewarded with a low chuckle.

"All in good time," the man said. "See the envelope? Open it."

As Paul reached into the locker to retrieve the envelope, I looked around. Somehow, this man was watching us. He knew we'd opened the locker. He knew where we were and what we were doing.

Paul extracted the envelope, his hands shaking slightly, and opened the flap to peer inside. A look of confusion crossed his face for a second before he upended the contents onto the worn tiles at our feet.

A newspaper clipping, a folded piece of paper, and a photograph fell out. Bending for a closer look, I read the headline aloud, "Local Girl Killed in Hit and Run: No Suspects Found."

"Ring any bells?" the voice on the phone hissed. My blood ran cold. No. No, this couldn't be happening. I ignored his question and reached for the folded piece of paper. It was a poster of Miranda Elliot, a young girl who was killed in a hit-and-run nearly twenty years ago. Under Miranda's photo, the local police department had made a plea for any information leading to the arrest and conviction of the driver from that night.

I cast a sideways glance at Paul, my palms sweaty. He looked ill, his face pasty and pale. We remained silent, yet our eyes spoke volumes as we caught each other's gazes.

This is worse than we thought. Much worse.

"Your silence says everything I need to know," the man growled into the phone. "It was your silence all those years ago that caused my sister to die as well. Miranda was walking to a friend's house but did she make it? No, because some sick drunk fuck ran her over with his truck and then covered it up. Ring any bells now, Paul?"

At this point, Paul was no longer even trying to hide his emotions. The accident senior year had plagued us our entire marriage. Paul had never gotten over that night, driving recklessly after a football game. God... I can still remember the thudding feeling of her body crushing under the wheels. It happened so fast.

Paul and I had been headed back to my house to mess around because my parents were out of town. There we were, speeding down Tar Creek Road, his hand up my skirt, empty beer bottles rolling around in the floor well. I remember leaning over to kiss him when all of a sudden he swerved but it was too late. We'd hit a deer.

But it wasn't a deer.

A young teenage girl lay in a crumpled heap on the gravel road. When I close my eyes I can still see the dark smear of blood she left behind in the red glow of the truck's tail lights. I can still hear the strangled garling sound she made as she tried to suck air into her crushed chest. I remember her eyes were opened, panicked, yet staring at nothing.

It was the worst moment of my life to that point.

Paul had gone into full panic mode then: pacing back and forth, running his hands through his hair frantically, muttering "Oh god, oh god," over and over. I pulled out my cell phone to call 911 only for him to snatch it away.

"What are you doing?" he yelled incredulously, his breath coming out in frenzied gulps.

"Calling for help!" I yelled, trying to snatch my phone back. He just held it higher, over his head. "She needs help! Paul! She needs help!"

"She's past helping, Heather. Look at her," Paul sobbed, glancing in the direction of the girl but not looking at her directly. "Oh my god... They'll put me in prison. And you too, probably."

"Me?" I screeched, "I'm not the idiot who hit her!" Of all the stupid things for him to say in a moment like that. He was more worried about saving his own hide than the young girl crumpled at his feet.

"Guilt by association, babe," Paul snapped condescendingly as though I was a child who didn't understand. "We have to get out of here. Cover our tracks and never speak of this again, got it?"

Suddenly, I was awash with fear again, but this time, it was for myself, for Paul. Would we go to prison? We were just kids ourselves; surely they wouldn't send us to prison. It was an accident!

Bile rose in my throat and I knew I was going to be sick, but before I could empty my stomach, Paul shoved his baseball cap under my face to catch it.

"We can't leave any evidence, okay? We were never here," he said softly, gently smoothing the damp strands of blond hair from my forehead. I remember him slowly leading me back to the cab of the truck, helping me into my seat, and leaning over me to buckle my seat belt. I closed my eyes when he got into the truck and shifted into reverse, slowly turning around and heading back the way we'd come.

The sight of the girl, broken and bloodied, in the eerie red glow of the taillights, as we left her there that night will forever haunt my dreams for years to come. In some sick and twisted way, that nightmare had brought Paul and me closer together. She was the secret we'd shared all these years.

Until now.

"If you would have just called 911, maybe Miranda would still be alive," the man's voice seethed over the phone. "Better yet, maybe if you wouldn't have been a total piece of shit human and oh... I don't know... driving drunk, then maybe Miranda would still be alive."

"What do you want from us?" Paul sucked in a breath as he tried to manage his emotions. I'd known him long enough to tell that he was barely hanging on. It was taking all of his willpower not to explode. "What can we do to make this right and get Caroline back?"

"That's the thing. You really can't, now can you? Nothing you can do will bring back my sister. But your silence all these years needs to end."

"You don't have any proof of any of this. You're just a sicko, trying to play mind games with people and kidnap kids," Paul spat, his voice full of false bravado. I sucked in a quiet breath, eyes round with alarm. If he angered this man further, would it cause him to harm Caroline, if he hadn't already? New worries began swirling in my head, pulsing through my chest with every beat of my heart. Dear god, I was going to pass out. This can't be happening.

I reached over and grabbed Paul's hand for support, but he gently shoved it away as he stood up and began to pace the aisle of worn-out lockers. The flickering light overhead was enough to make me want to scream. Suddenly the buzzing sound emitting from the fluorescent lighting changed octaves becoming even more grating.

"Oh, I assure you, I have proof. How else do you think I tracked you down after all these years, Paul?" the man laughed, his voice laced with smugness.

"Let us talk to Caroline!" Paul roared, coming to a halt and glaring down at the phone. His face was red and a vein throbbed in his forehead.

"Or what?" the man snapped. "Look, I don't take orders from you. You take them from me. Do you want to see your daughter again? Let's play another game."

My stomach instantly began churning again, wondering what level of sick depravity he'd come up with. He had us by the throat and he knew it. If we wanted to see our sweet, innocent Caroline again, we had to do whatever he demanded, no matter how twisted.

"Three blocks south, two blocks east. Green dumpster in the alley. You'll find an address. Go to that address. You have thirty minutes." The call disconnected.

Paul and I stared at each other, our minds processing what we'd just been told before we finally snapped out of it. I shoved the items back inside the envelope and, taking it with me, we ran for our car. I'm not sure why I took it all with me. Perhaps, in that moment, it felt like some demented tie to Caroline. Or, more likely, I was hoping to give it to the police as evidence to apprehend our child's kidnapper once we got her back.

Except we couldn't do that, could we? Then we'd have to explain our involvement with the kidnapper and his family from all those years ago.

Racing down the slippery wet marble steps of Grigby Station, Paul and I frantically made it to our car in record time. The misty rain from moments ago had turned into a soaking downpour and I was instantly cold and wet.

"Okay, he said two blocks south..." Paul mumbled, pulling out onto the street.

"Three. It was three south, two east," I corrected him, firm in my answer. He turned and looked at me as though to question me. "I'm sure, Paul. Now is not the time. I wouldn't chance my daughter's safety."

"Your daughter?" he snapped, suddenly getting belligerent. "She's my daughter too, you know."

"Yes, Paul, I'm aware," I glared at him. *Was he really going to do this right now?* Of all the times in our marriage, this was the time we needed to work together.

"Well, you said, 'your daughter,'" he accused as he passed through the second intersection.

"I didn't mean it in any way to upset you. Good grief," I huffed, getting more and more angry at him. If it wasn't for him, we wouldn't even be in this situation to begin with!

"Well, all I'm saying is—"

"Turn here," I interrupted him as we entered the third southward intersection. I didn't have the mental space to deal with his sensitive emotions at that moment. "We go two blocks this way and then we stop and look for a green dumpster."

***

Moments later, we approached the second intersection headed east and Paul pulled over. He got out of the car, slamming his door with a little more force than needed. I sighed inwardly as I quickly climbed out of the car and headed for the nearest alley.

The rain continued to pour as I swiftly made my way to the mouth of the alley, dodging puddles as I went. It was a useless effort, of course, as I was already drenched.

Paul, with his sulking attitude, had run across the intersection to the other alley looking for a green dumpster. Irritated by his sudden change in attitude, I pressed on, slipping into the shadows of the alley. Almost too late, I began worrying about getting mugged or attacked down some seedy alleyway by myself. Afraid I was two seconds away from becoming a main character on a Dateline episode, but even more afraid for my daughter's safety, I steeled my spine with grim determination. I would not be fearful.

From the dim haze cast from the streetlights behind me, I could see at least four dumpsters. The first two were blue, the next one was red, and brown after that. Trash lay scattered around the base of the red one as though someone, or something, had dug through it. I willed myself to not think about what kind of creature could be lurking in its depths.

Turning on the flashlight application on my phone, I cast its small light around the darkened alleyway, hoping to illuminate a green dumpster. It was as though I could feel the clock ticking down the seconds with every beat of my heart. What would happen to Caroline if we were late? Would he kill her out of spite? Or was he just being an asshole, taunting us with a past that we couldn't change?

I had suggested to Paul numerous times throughout the years that we should go to the police and tell them everything. Then maybe I'd sleep better at night. Maybe he'd be less anxious.

He always said no.

As I made my way down the alleyway now, I mulled over the options in my head, determining in my heart that enough was enough. If it wasn't for Paul's silence, and his recklessness, then we wouldn't be in this situation. If

I hadn't been quiet about it all then perhaps Caroline wouldn't have been taken.

"No green dumpsters that way," Paul's voice suddenly came up behind me, causing me to jump. I hadn't even heard him approach. I paused long enough for him to walk alongside me as we slowly made our way deeper into the shadows.

"We're almost to the end. Are you sure this is the right one?" he asked, looking farther ahead as best he could in the limited light.

Suddenly, something large fell to our right, causing a loud metal clanking sound, causing us both to jump to attention. I caught sight of the back end of a ginger cat, tail puffed out, as it made a mad dash down the alleyway beyond. An overturned trash can lay on its side, trash strewn everywhere.

It was what was sitting behind the trash can, deep in the shadows, within a recess of the brick building on the right side of the alley that caught my eye. Under an old, soiled mattress, that may or may not have been part of a crime scene, sat a rusted green dumpster.

"There!" I exclaimed, already making my way toward it. Sidestepping the detritus, I bent to check the exterior of the dumpster for any signs of the mystery address that the kidnapper had mentioned.

I could feel Paul beside me as he, too, looked for the address. Seeing nothing suspicious on the front or left side of the metal dumpster, I cringed internally as I watched him pull the sodden 'murder mattress' off. What horrors were we going to find inside?

Throwing the mattress behind him, Paul immediately tore at the thick black plastic lid of the dumpster. It wouldn't open.

"What the hell..." he continued shaking the lid, trying the clasp. Anger evident on his face, he kicked the dumpster, causing a loud banging sound. About that time, I noticed the padlock.

"There must be a key," I pointed to the lock, "or, the address we need will be on the outside."

"Or he never intended for us to win this challenge," Paul growled as he began pulling the metal beast of a trash bin out from its place against the brick wall. With a grunt, he pulled it out enough to shimmy behind it.

"See anything?" I asked, watching him as he squeezed his large frame behind the dumpster. His eyes roamed the rusted surface and he shook his head.

"Noth–" he suddenly stopped, evidently finding something of interest. He bent then and when he stood, he was holding a key. "It was dangling on a small hook near the bottom."

"Here, hand it over," I held out my hand and he dropped it in. While he climbed out from behind the dumpster, I immediately went to work on the lock.

Within seconds, the lock sprung open, and I ripped the right side of the lid back, revealing the contents of the dumpster.

Inside, illuminated by my cell phone, lay my daughter's denim jacket. I almost dropped my phone as my hands began trembling and a sob escaped my lips. Where was Caroline? My dear, sweet Caroline?

Paul rushed to my side to peer in, and he too let out a feral moan. Were we too late? Where was this address we were meant to find?

I reached for her jacket and, bringing it to my face, inhaled the scent of her: soap, vanilla, her favorite shampoo… Tears began to fall in earnest now. I was broken. A mother who doesn't know where to find her child is as lost as a wave who can't find the shore… it just isn't natural. It shouldn't happen.

"Check her pockets. For the address."

Snapping out of my fugue, I quickly obliged but found nothing except a used tissue, a hair tie, and a quarter. "Nothing," I cried miserably.

"It has to be here," Paul growled in frustration. He stuck his head deeper into the half-full dumpster, muttering to himself. The stench of the garbage increased as he began moving bags around, looking for the address.

"Here, I'll help," I offered as I slipped on Caroline's jacket. I didn't want to lay it on the wet, disgusting alleyway floor and besides, I was wet to the bone.

Stepping around Paul, I lifted the second black plastic lid on the dumpster and gasped. There, taped on the underside, was another Manilla envelope.

"Paul!" I ripped it away from the lid, my hands leaving wet marks on the dry paper. Shaking now, from being chilled or from the sheer emotional turmoil this night had turned into I don't know. I hastily tore at the closure of the envelope, yanking the little metal clasp loose in the process.

Inside was a single sheet of printer paper. On it, written in black Sharpie, was a message:

"168 Slokum Rd, warehouse B2, back entrance. 20 mins"

"Slokum Road... isn't that out by the old glass plant?" I asked Paul, my mind going in fifty different directions. It wasn't too far away from where we were, but twenty minutes wasn't a long time.

"Among other things," Paul nodded, grabbing my hand as he headed back toward the mouth of the alley. I ran alongside him, dodging puddles and wayward pieces of trash as I went, eager to get back to the car.

***

As we raced down the road, headed towards the industrial end of town, my mind continued to work overtime. I was mentally and physically exhausted but the sheer anxiety and fear surrounding me like a vice seemed to only tighten with every beat of my heart. Suddenly I felt as though I couldn't breathe, as though someone was sitting on my chest. Now was not a time to have a panic attack. I had to calm down.

Rolling down my window for some fresh air rewarded me with rain droplets making their way through the opening and cooling my heated face. Even though I was already soaking wet from walking around in the alley, the cool raindrops now brought blessed relief to my overheated anxiety-ridden skin.

Following the GPS, Paul slowed the car as we neared 168 Slokum Road, home to a long-abandoned industrial park. The large, empty buildings stood sentinel against the night sky, as rain continued to pound against their rusted roofs. The parking lot and driveway, once nicely graveled, were now dotted with tall weeds and detritus. Graffitied walls brought the only array of color I could see from my vantage point to the dismal environment. What was left of the chain link fence surrounding the industrial park appeared to be cut or sagging, at least the part I could see in the car's headlight beams.

"This is... depressing," I commented, still taking it all in. Everything outside my window was pitch black except for the area illuminated directly under two weak streetlights farther across the gravel lot.

"And creepy as hell," Paul agreed as we slowly pulled around the first building in search of warehouse B2. The sound of the gravel crunching under our tires competed with the light drum of rain hitting the car's roof. If it wasn't for our daughter being kidnapped, the sound might almost be relaxing.

Something scurried past us, just outside the headlight beam, causing Paul to slam on the brakes. I grabbed the dashboard out of reflex, my nerves frayed beyond their limit. My heart seemed to pound out of my chest, just as it had since I'd received that initial call from that hideous man. How long was that sustainable before I had a heart attack and dropped dead? Then what good would I be to my daughter?

As we circled behind the first building, two more came into view, each one in the same state of disrepair as the first. Peeling blue paint and rust covered the metal exterior of the old warehouses. What few windows I could see all appeared to be busted out. The shards of glass, glistening in the beam of the headlights, lay scattered below on the gravel parking lot. Halfway up the side of one of the buildings was a large white square with a black 'B1' painted in the center of it.

I pointed it out to Paul. At least now we knew what type of markings we were looking for. It didn't take long before we found it: B2.

The building was almost identical to B1 except there was a light on over the back door. All the other buildings were dark. B2 was beckoning us.

Paul pulled to a stop and, with an anxious sigh, parked and got out. I was quick to follow, not sure what we'd find inside.

The rusted metal door groaned in protest as I pulled it open with effort and we made our way inside. The inky blackness instantly engulfed us, causing me to be on edge. Was the kidnapper here, lurking in the shadows, ready to attack? And where was Caroline?

Turning the light on my phone again, I willed my battery not to die. I'd charged my phone in the car so hopefully it would last. Waiting for Paul to follow suit, we slowly made our way deeper into the bowels of the building.

Rain echoed on the old tin roof, the sound reverberating off of the vaulted ceiling. Through the dim shadows, I could just make out some kind of machinery and gray metal shelving. Puddles lay scattered across the floor, made from dripping pipes or the rusted roof above. A strong scent of damp and mildew assaulted our noses.

"What now?" I whispered to Paul, uncertain if we were fully alone, but sure that we were being watched nonetheless. There, at a minimum, had to be a camera hidden somewhere. How else had this madman been keeping track of our whereabouts all night?

"I'm not sure, but I don't have a good feeling about this," Paul replied quietly, casting his light about the room. "This whole thing is messed up."

Just then, my phone's screen lit up and the ringtone shattered the relative silence, causing Paul and I to jump. Shakily, I pressed the button to answer the call and placed it on speakerphone.

"Ahhh.... So nice that you made it in time," the kidnapped cooed, his voice as unappealing as wet hair in a shower drain. I tried not to shudder as a chill coursed down my spine. My heart rate, still not recovered from the evening's earlier events, began climbing again at the mere sound of his wretched voice.

"When do we get to see Caroline?" I demanded, not interested in playing his games any further. I wanted to see my daughter *now.*

"There's one more thing that must be done. The whole point to all of this," the kidnapper said coldly, sending another chill down my spine. "Paul, as we discussed earlier, your silence, your... inability to take ownership of your actions, ends tonight."

Paul looked at me nervously, sweat beading up on his brow. I gave him what I hoped was an encouraging look. I'm guessing I failed because he quickly looked away and wouldn't find my gaze again.

"Paul, if you want to see your daughter again, you will call the police and confess your sins. Tell them everything: how you were driving drunk, how you ran through a car wash on the way home that night to wash away evidence, how you went into the collision repair shop claiming you'd hit a deer. That's when you made your mistake, by the way. You thought you'd be smart and go three towns over to get that dented bumper fixed. What you didn't expect was for the mechanic to find a clump of hair stuck in the underside of the bumper. He didn't know if it was important, so he saved it. Well, he didn't watch the news and no one showed up at the garage asking questions because it sat in his drawer for years. That is until I showed up, looking for information about my sister's death."

Paul sucked in an audible breath at the revelation and I felt him stiffen next to me. I'm not quite sure how I felt at that moment: anxious? relieved? afraid? My whole marriage and relationship with Paul had been overshadowed by that night. That one cool night so long ago. But what would happen now? If the cops came and arrested Paul for killing Miranda, what would happen to Ava and Caroline? What would happen to me? Would I end up in prison, just like Paul told me I would?

"Paul, you must take out your phone and call the police now. Confess your sins and then, before they get here, you can be reunited with your daughter."

"That's it? I confess and you'll let us have Caroline back?" Paul asked, his voice cracking.

"I'm a man of my word, Paul. Call the police now while I'm still on the line with Heather. I want to hear you," the kidnapper commanded in a condescending voice.

I stood there, in the cool, damp warehouse, anxiously waiting for my husband to make the call. My hands shook uncontrollably. This moment, this second in time, would alter the course of our lives, one way or another, and I didn't know if I was ready for it. I just wanted to hold my daughter in my arms. I wanted to wipe the tears from her cheeks. I wanted to hear her laugh.

With a deep sigh of resignation, lips in a grim line, Paul pulled out his cell phone and began dialing. I could hear the operator on the other end answer and then Paul began to speak. His voice started quiet, broken, and then as he continued, it grew firmer and more confident, as though he knew our daughter's life depended on his confession.

As he stood there beside me, relaying the ugly, horrible things that had happened that night so long ago, I felt something shift in our relationship. For years now, I'd let the dark seed of resentment grow and fester, marring our relationship with its hideousness. That night has hung over our heads like rot, slowly eating us away.

As he relayed to the detective the sins of the past, I felt as though a weight was being lifted, as though we were set free.

A few moments later, Paul finished his confession and hung up. Turning to me, tears in his eyes, he murmured, "They will be here soon. After that, I don't know what will happen. Please tell the girls I love them."

A sob escaped my throat as the full gravity of the situation fell on my shoulders. What *would* happen?

"I did what you wanted, so where is Caroline?" Paul nearly spat into my phone as we anxiously awaited the arrival of the police. We must hurry, as we only had moments.

"Well done, Paul. Didn't think you'd have it in you if we're being honest," the kidnapper's deep chuckle flooded over the phone's speaker. "I guess that means you and Heather get a chance to see sweet Caroline again."

"What do you mean 'chance'?" my voice climbed an octave from rising anxiety. He said we'd get Caroline back if we talked to the police! Not that we'd get a *chance* to see her!

"I was going to play one last game with Paul since he was just a brave, brave boy, but I've been thinking…" The condescension of the kidnapper seemed to know no bounds. "I've decided to up the ante, if you will."

I felt like vomiting again. How much more stress could my poor system take before I finally collapsed under mental and physical duress?

A deep laugh filled the room as it echoed across my phone. The kidnapper seemed to think it was great fun watching parents having a mental breakdown while he toyed with them.

Suddenly, at the end of a short corridor ahead of us, a television screen turned on, emitting an eerie blue glow. As we watched, a man's face appeared on the screen. He wore all black, including the mask covering his face's upper half. His blond hair was slicked back with too much gel to the point I began wondering if it was even real. The only part of his actual body I could see were his eyes: blue, cold, and dead inside.

"Hiya folks," he greeted as though he were about to sell us a used Subaru, instead of being the sick bastard who kidnapped our oldest daughter. He'd been watching us all night, just like we'd suspected, but where was he now? Was he hidden somewhere in the shadows of the warehouse or tucked away in some other unassuming location?

I could only glare at him through the screen, my energy already sapped from me. Paul, on the other hand, tensed and acted like he was about to lunge at the television.

"Wouldn't do that, Pauly," the kidnapper crooned with a wag of his long, bony finger. "You see, if something happens to me, then you'll never find Caroline in time, right?" That last part caused Paul to pause and the kidnapper seemed pleased as evidenced by his toothy, snake-like smile.

"Tell you what? I'm feeling... generous tonight. Since you've both played along so well, I'm going to let you each pick a room. You know, double your chances of seeing your daughter again." He paused for a moment, appearing thoughtful. "There are six offices upstairs in this warehouse, meaning there are six doors to choose from. Open the correct door if you want to see your daughter's face again."

Paul and I stood there, confused, waiting for the punchline of the sick joke we found ourselves in. When we didn't move fast enough, the man rolled his eyes and lunged at us through the screen, "Go!"

I grabbed my husband's hand and we quickly climbed the stairs. I wondered if he could feel my hands shaking like I could feel his. As we arrived at the top of the stairs, Paul began reaching for the nearest door, but I stopped him.

"Wait! We each only get one chance. One door. Shouldn't we talk this through first, you know, strategize a little?" I asked, looking around at my surroundings.

The upstairs of the building looked like it had been deserted for quite some time. It smelled musty with a hint of something unpleasant akin to rotten vegetables. Like broccoli that's been kept in the refrigerator too long and has become soupy. The cement floors were dirty, with piles of trash or empty beer cans scattered randomly throughout the deserted area. In the distance, I could hear water dripping. All the pipes that I could see, which weren't many, were all corroded and rusty. The cinder block walls were stained in areas from where the rusted water pipes had leaked through the years.

At least that's what I hoped it was.

"So what do you think we should do?" Paul asked, following my line of sight. "Knock on the doors and listen for her to make a sound?"

"Eeny meeny?" I mumbled, using my dark humor as a coping method. I could feel Paul's scowl without even looking at him.

Suddenly, the lights flickered and went out, leaving us in complete darkness. As if we hadn't already been through an emotional roller coaster, but now we were in the pitch dark.

"What the—" Paul began but drew up short when suddenly a static sound could be heard from somewhere to our left.

Blinded by the inky darkness, I turned to the sound like it was a lifeline. *What was going on? Who was there? Was it Caroline?*

The static stopped just as suddenly as it started and I began to breathe again. But just as I began to feel even a modicum of relief in the pitch black, suddenly Neil Diamond's voice began pouring out of hidden speakers. *Sweet Caroline* played loudly all around us, disorienting us. It was horrifying. The music was so loud I couldn't hear my heartbeat.

Reaching out for Paul, for his warm presence, I felt nothing but cool air. Where was he? Where was... anything? As the song began playing on repeat, I began to sob, reaching out to find anything to anchor myself to.

Snot and tears poured down my face as I continued to feel around myself. Slowly moving my feet, I shuffled a few steps but felt nothing. The music still assaulted my ears. I cried out for Paul even though I knew it was futile. If I couldn't even hear myself scream, how could he possibly hear me?

When I thought all was lost, suddenly the music switched off and the lights flickered on, but not the normal overhead lights from before. This time, it was black lights.

All along the hallway, strips of black lights hung, casting a strange purple glow. On the doors to the different rooms, someone had crudely painted numbers. Until the black light had turned on, I hadn't noticed the numbers but there they were in various neon colors.

"Look at this," Paul called from somewhere behind me. I turned then and saw him looking at a now-visible sign that read, "Pick a number for a chance to win!"

"So not only is this guy a psycho, he's a smart ass, too?" I muttered as I leaned in to inspect the message. I touched it and noticed the edges of the paint were still tacky.

"It's still wet," I whispered, "You think he's here somewhere, watching us?"

"I'll fucking kill him if he is," Paul growled, casting a glare around us.

"We have to find Caroline first," I cautioned. "And we have to hurry. The police will be here any moment."

"We find Caroline, *then* we find him," Paul agreed, moving down the hall. "I'll take door number two." He paused outside the door with the neon pink two sloppily painted on it and waited for me to make my selection.

The speakers began to static again and Sweet Caroline began playing again but this time Neil Diamond's voice had been replaced with a creepy, child-like voice. The kind I'd heard in countless horror movies throughout the years. The music accompanying the singing wasn't the typical music either. This time it had been replaced by some kind of slow, broken jewelry box sound. If it weren't for the dire situation I found myself in, I'd probably have laughed at the sheer theatrics of it all.

Trying to ignore the onslaught of garish music pumping through the hidden speakers surrounding Paul and me, I knew I had a decision to make. A decision that could very well stand in between my seeing my daughter dead or alive again. After a moment's hesitation, I made my decision.

I slowly made my way to the door marked number four. I'm not sure why I picked four, but it seemed right. I turned to Paul, my hand on the knob. With a nod to each other, we turned our door knobs and opened our doors.

Inside my room of choice was pitch black. The eerie glow from the blacklight in the hallway barely cast a whisper of a shadow within the small room. The only thing I could make out in the shadows was the fact that the room was tiny and empty except for a large box in the middle of the floor.

Feeling around on either side of the doorway for a possible light switch, I found none. Sighing, I shuffled through the darkness, trying to make my way to the box. To Caroline. Was she inside?

The confounded music continued to play, blaring and unrelenting. As I was stumbling across the dark room, I was suddenly assaulted by a strobe light going off overhead. Stunted by two of my senses–sound and now sight–I found myself on the edge of tears again as I approached within arms reach of the large box in the middle of the room.

It was a wooden crate, its surface rough to the touch. Standing approximately five feet tall and four feet wide, it was large enough to hold Caroline. Dear, sweet Caroline.

"Caroline?" I yelled over the din of the monstrous rendition of Neil Diamond's classic. How could I expect my daughter to hear me when I couldn't even hear myself calling out to her?

Through the flashing strobe light over my head, I reached out and began tugging at the front of the crate. The strobe caused everything to appear in choppy movement and I was starting to get a headache.

Trying to ignore the insistent sound of the music pulsing through my ears and the constant flashing of the lights, I continued pulling at the wooden boards that made up the crate. Splinters dug into my skin, jabbing under my fingernails, but still, I pressed on, pulling and tugging at the wood.

I felt the rough board give in my hands. Elation pulsed through me as I gave it another tug and felt it come loose. With another tug, the other end of the board freed itself and revealed the dark interior of the crate.

I could see Caroline's hair! She seemed to be lying on the bottom of the crate, unmoving. He must have drugged her and kept her inside the crate for his own sick game.

"Caroline!" I screamed to be heard over the din of the racket pulsing from the hidden speakers. She didn't move. Frustrated, I reached into the void I'd made, feeling for my daughter's hair. The strobe light continued to disorient me, causing everything to seem surreal.

My hand made contact with her scalp, and in that blessed moment, tears filled my eyes. My dear, sweet Caroline! I'd found her!

But something was wrong. She didn't seem to respond to my touch. No. No, this couldn't be happening. Surely she was just drugged.

Fear and panic pumped through my veins yet again, while bile rose in my throat. I began kicking at the boards of the crate in a frenzied attack. Sweat began pouring down my spine, dripping down my forehead, but still, I pressed on. I had to get to Caroline.

The bottom board finally gave way under my foot, the board splintering and fracturing in two. Immediately dropping to my knees, I leaned in to get a better view but the horror I saw had me scrambling backwards.

Through the pulsing of the strobe light overhead, my eyes relayed a message to my brain that I was unwilling to accept. For laying in the bottom of the crate was the bloodied, severed head of my sweet Caroline.

A wail built in my chest, pulling from every aspect of my being. As the reality began to set in, my sorrow erupted in the most harrowing sound I've ever heard. For the first time since that confounded song had started to play so loudly, so unrelenting, I could hear something else. My screams.

Suddenly feeling ill, I stood weakly and stumbled toward the opened door. I made it all of two steps before I vomited the contents of my stomach and began dry heaving, pictures of Caroline's head flashing through my head.

Dead God... how would we get through this? How would we explain it to Ava? How did I tell Paul?

Once the heaving subsided, I slowly headed to the corridor to find my husband.

As I stepped outside the room, the music abruptly stopped. The sudden quiet was just as disorienting and jarring as the unrelenting noise had been. I could hear my heartbeat again, and my ragged breath. Tears still streamed down my cheeks as I thought about what I'd just seen; about my dear sweet daughter, slaughtered for the enjoyment of some sick monster.

Paul was standing at the end of the corridor, in front of door number two, a look of deep sorrow etched on his face. How did he know already? Had he heard me scream?

As I got closer to Paul, I could see that his eyes were red from crying, his face swollen. When he saw me approach, he eyed me wearily, as though gauging my reaction.

"I found her, Heather," he sobbed, "I found Caroline." *What's left of her, that is*, I thought darkly, anger churning in my stomach once again.

"Well, well...." the speakers rattled to life again. "It appears you chose wisely after all." The deep, raspy laugh I'd become accustomed to filled the hallway. "Way to go, Paul and Heather!" Sarcasm dripped from his voice. I could hear a few clicking sounds, and then nothing but static.

"You lied to us!" Paul yelled. Turning to me, desperation and grief etched into his face, he wailed, "The mother fucker lied to us!"

"No, Paul, he didn't," I said, as an eerie calm washed over me. Perhaps it was shock kicking in. "He didn't lie to us."

"Yes, he did! He told us we could see Caroline again," Paul insisted, his breathing rough and ragged. "He told us he'd let us see her."

"And he did," I let out a sob, the true horror of the situation burning deep in my chest, "He just never said alive."

2

THE BLIZZARD

The snow continued to fall, swirling and churning, a white fury of cold flakes that melted as soon as they touched my windshield. I turned the wipers on the highest setting to wipe away the winter slush accumulating on the glass and obscuring my view. It felt like we were crawling along the highway. I had to go faster, had to put some more miles between me and him, but the blizzard and the darkness seemed to have other plans.

I glanced in my rearview mirror. No headlights following me that I could see. Just pitch black save for the eerie red glow from my tail lights on the snow. I nervously looked back to the road ahead and then in the rearview mirror again, this time catching the view of my sleeping daughter, nestled warm and safe, in her car seat. She was the reason I had to get away. But I knew he'd follow. It was only a matter of time before he realized we were gone.

I didn't have a choice, you see, so before you judge me, hear me out. I didn't choose this life. Well, maybe I did at some level. But I didn't want it all to turn out this way.

I met my husband in college. I was working as a waitress, trying to make some extra cash just to get by. He'd come into the diner, a small greasy spoon off of Route 72, one rainy night right before closing. I remember cringing when I heard the bell over the door ding, announcing his arrival. I was tired, headachy, and had a midterm the following morning that I wasn't quite prepared for. I just wanted to go home. But, alas, I was a poor college student in need of tips so I plastered on a smile and turned to greet my guest.

His eyes are what attracted me to him first— blue. He was tall, dark-haired, and very attractive even though he was soaking wet from the deluge outside.

"What can I get for you? We are closing soon and the cook has already closed up the kitchen for the night. I might be able to scrounge something up for you though," I greeted, cringing when I caught myself babbling.

He smiled at me, revealing a row of straight white teeth. "Just coffee if you have it, please." He took off his jacket and shook it lightly over the rug by the door. I nodded and headed for the kitchen. I could handle coffee surely. I quickly set the machine to brew and went back out to the dining room.

I found him sitting at one of the chipped formica tables near the jukebox. Setting down a plate holding a glazed doughnut from out of the display case near the register, I said, "You need something to go with coffee on a night like tonight." A crack of lightning flashed overhead right then, almost as if on cue, causing us to jump. We both started laughing. He picked up the doughnut with a smile and I headed to get the coffee.

As I poured his cup of coffee, I handed him a container of various pre-measured flavored creamers and sugar packets. "Thanks," he smiled, digging through and selecting some hazelnut creamer. "I'm Dean."

"Abby," I smiled. "Nice to meet you. Just let me know if you need anything else."

"Thanks for the doughnut. Do you bake them yourself?" he asked, pointing to a sign on the smudged display case that announced that the doughnuts were baked fresh daily using locally sourced ingredients.

"Ha! No!" I laughed. I looked around conspiratorially and added, "And I have it on good authority that they aren't baked fresh daily nor their ingredients locally sourced... unless that's what you call buying them off the discount rack at the grocery store."

Dean busted up laughing at that. "Really? Well, isn't that false advertisement?" he grinned.

"You apparently haven't met the boss man," I grinned, rolling my eyes and stifling a laugh. "He makes us wrap the doughnuts up in a damp paper towel and microwave them for 30 seconds every morning to "freshen them up" as he calls it."

Dean looked down at the half of the doughnut he still held in his hand. He pointed to it while he chewed. "You did that?"

"Guilty as charged," I sighed, holding out my wrists to feign being handcuffed.

"Well, the boss might be a cheapskate but I guess it works. It wasn't that bad."

"But it wasn't that good either," I quipped as we both started laughing. It was then, in that shared moment, that I felt a connection to Dean. Apparently, he felt it too because we sat there for the next few hours, talking late into the night.

We were pretty much inseparable from there on out, getting married just 6 months later.

I know, you can't know somebody that well after just six months, but I was young, naive, and thought I knew what was best.

At first, everything seemed to go well. I moved out of the dorm and into his little house on Maple St. I was still in school so we decided that I should focus on my studies and he would work to cover the mortgage and bills. I only had a few semesters left and then I would hopefully get a job using my degree—early childhood education.

I poured my energy into studying which sometimes caused the housework to be lacking. It was only a few months into the marriage when the comments started, snide and demeaning. "Maybe you should take fewer classes so you can clean up a little around here." or "I've been working all day and I have to come home to this?" or "You can't even make something hot for dinner?"

I would typically get upset, as anyone would, and try to hide the tears as I would attempt to come up with something for dinner. Something quick to lessen his negative mood. Sometimes he caught me crying.

"Seriously? You're crying?" he'd sneer. I'd just keep my back to him when I could. I was doing the best I could but no matter what I did, it was never good enough, fast enough, clean enough. At first, I would try to defend myself, explaining about the term papers due or the upcoming tests. He would always just stare at me as though he was looking right through me. Like I wasn't even there.

The first physical attack occurred around our first anniversary. I remember standing in the laundry room, matching socks when he got home early one evening.

"Dinner isn't ready yet?" he asked, coming up behind me. I jumped, startled, as I hadn't heard him come home.

"Oh! I was thinking of doing baked chicken tonight," I said brightly, feigning a smile. "I wasn't expecting you home so early. I can start dinner now though."

"Yeah, maybe you should," he snapped, rolling his eyes at me. He stalked off towards the kitchen and I heard him open the refrigerator door, rummaging around. It slammed shut, hard, and before I could react, he appeared in the laundry room doorway again. "Where's my beer? You were supposed to get more at the store," he growled accusingly.

"I'm sorry. I must have forgotten to get more today. I ran into Vicky from down the street and we got to talking," I apologized.

He took a step towards me, coming fully into the stuffy laundry room, and blocking my exit.

"How many times have I told you that you better keep the fridge stocked for when I get home?" he growled. "I work all day long, dealing with idiots, and I have to come home to this?"

I took a step backward, trying to put as much distance between him and me, and felt the top edge of the dryer digging into my hip. "I said I was sorry. I can—"

It was then that his fist connected with my jaw, causing me to see stars. The pain was instantaneous, and I put my hands up defensively, unsure if or when another blow was coming. I could taste the iron in my mouth, the blood beginning to flow from where I'd bit my tongue. I felt tears, some from pain, some from anger, begin pooling in my eyes and I willed them not to fall. He would love that. Love to see me cry so that he could mock me, and belittle me. I looked down at the floor, unwilling to make eye contact with him. I could hear his breathing, rapid and deep. Could feel his eyes on me, angry and hard.

"I'm tired of your excuses," he said, leaning forward to whisper in my ear, pressing his body against mine. "Maybe if you weren't such a pathetic excuse for a wife, you'd remember something as simple as beer." He then punched the wall near my head to make me jump. He started laughing as he pushed away from me. "What an idiot," he mumbled as he left the room. I stood there, petrified and unmoving, as I listened to him grab his keys from the dish near the door and then slam the door behind him. I felt like I didn't breathe again until I heard his truck fire up outside in the driveway and then pull away down the road with a squeal of tires and flinging rocks.

Now, I found myself driving down this deserted high-way in the middle of a blizzard with my child in the back seat. Because the violence didn't stop that day in the laundry room. It just got worse. And when my daughter was born, it still didn't stop. I knew I had to get away–get her away– from him.

I knew he'd come after us. I quickly glanced in the rearview mirror again at the thought. Still nothing. I relaxed a little at that but then tensed again as the car swerved sideways on the icy road. Quickly righting the vehicle, I carefully pulled back into the middle of the roadway. We were on a two-lane deserted highway in the middle of nowhere. Driving down the middle was okay to me in a blizzard like this. I'd caught views of deep gaping ravines on either side of the asphalted road and I did not want to slide into one. The swirling snow continued falling, blowing across the beams of my dimmed headlights. The white precipitation was already accumulating on the hood and headlights of my car and I started second-guessing my decision to bring my child out on a night like this. But then I thought about the alternative. Being at his mercy. Putting her in danger.

I thought that when she was born maybe he'd have a change of heart and stop hurting me. Boy, had I been wrong. If anything, the violence had gotten worse, him taking his anger and frustration at her colicky cries out on me. I watched him like a hawk, looking for any signs that he was going to hurt her but I saw nothing. It seemed that he would just take it all out on me. Not that I was okay with that–I wasn't okay with any of it–but at least it was me and not her. She brought joy to my life that I had never known. A love so innocent, so pure, that nothing could take it away. I remembered holding her soft warm body, smoothing her barely-there wisps of hair. The scent of her milk breath was fresh and sweet. The sound of her newborn grunts and cooing. The toothless, gummy smile covered in drool. The little kicks and punches she made, trying to catch the dangling toys and mirrors of her floor toys.

I sighed now, driving down the treacherous road, thinking about those early days of motherhood. A glance in the rearview mirror again revealed that she was still sleeping soundly, oblivious to the chaos around her.

I had to find a place to stay, or a gas station at the least. I had some cash that I had been saving to use for our escape. Dean had controlled all the money, making it difficult for me to squirrel anything away for myself. He'd check receipts, and demand I use the credit card only. He said it was to keep a log of spending for tax purposes but I wasn't stupid. I knew he was watching me. I saved money for this escape very slowly. For one Christmas my mom had sent a Christmas card with a check for a few hundred dollars written out to me. I took it to a bank that we didn't usually use and cashed it, pocketing the money and then hiding it when I got home. Hopefully, my mom didn't ask Dean what we spent the money on because then he would know about it. Mom didn't like Dean much so my chances were pretty high that she wouldn't ask him.

I'm sure you're wondering why I didn't just call the cops or tell my family what was going on but it wasn't that simple. On the surface, Dean was the perfect husband, worked a nice job, and doted on his daughter. No one would have believed me. Surely his friends and coworkers would have sided with him. So would his family. My mom was the only family I had left and she wouldn't—couldn't—have believed me due to her early stages of dementia and the fact that she lived four states away with her husband, Cliff. My stepdad Cliff thought that Dean had walked on water. He wouldn't have believed me even if I showed him the bruises. My friends had all drifted away as adulthood and motherhood consumed their lives. I didn't have anyone to talk to but Dean and our baby. I was truly alone in this.

Chin up, I continued driving onward into the darkness. The car's heater hummed at full speed but a chill ran down my spine at the thought of him following us. What if he tried taking the baby from me? I glanced at the digital clock on the dashboard. The eerie green glow informed me that it was almost midnight. The gas gauge had dipped to a quarter of a tank. We'd been driving for a few hours already. I sighed, knowing that another tank of gas meant dipping into my meager stash of money again. When I had set out on this escape I hadn't planned for a blizzard. I was going to wait another month or so before making my move. But the fight this past morning as he left for work was the catalyst.

He had been holding the baby and singing to her when I walked into the kitchen. As I walked by him, he stuck out his foot. He started laughing when I tripped and fell into the fridge. I stood up and looked at him, disbelief and hurt evident on my face.

"What? Don't look at me like that," he said, acting innocently. "Maybe you should put your energy into watching where you're walking, huh?"

"You tripped me on purpose. Why are you so mean to me all the time?" I asked, anger boiling just under the surface. I schooled my emotions and tried to relax my face. I wouldn't— couldn't— let him see how he made me feel. It seemed to delight him. My pain, emotional or physical, was just fuel for his fire. He relished in it and I wasn't going to feed the inferno brewing deep in his dark soul.

"I didn't trip you, you dumb bitch!" he snarled, his face contorting into a twisted, red mess. "You're just worthless, like always. God, I can't believe how dumb you are and always trying to blame it on me!"

The open palm smack landed on my cheek, pushing my face sideways. I hadn't seen it coming even though I should have. Maybe I *was* an idiot. My hand reflectively covered my stinging cheek, my eyes watering, my breathing elevated. I turned to put some space between us when he reached out and grabbed my arm, his fingers digging into my flesh, and twirling me back around to face him.

"Where are you going? Off to hide in the bedroom again and cry? Look at me when I'm talking to you!" he screamed, yanking my arm harder. Just then our daughter started crying, her wails making my heart hurt. I tried reaching for her to soothe her. He yanked her away from my grasp. Her cries became more urgent and again I reached for her.

"Shut up, you little bitch! You're no better than your worthless mother!" Dean spat as he held our daughter precariously in one arm while squeezing my arm with his other hand. His angry words just caused the toddler's howls to escalate and he shook her. Getting frustrated, he finally shoved her at me.

"Make her shut up!" he growled. I snatched our daughter and swiftly retreated from the kitchen, shushing her as

I went. A few moments later, I felt the wall shake slightly as the front door slammed shut and he left.

He's never hurt the baby that I knew of, never screamed at her the way he just did. But I was done making excuses for him. He'd crossed a line. It was bad enough that he was constantly yelling and belittling me, smacking me, leaving bruises where no one else could see. but to treat my daughter like that? No way in Hell could I allow that. I decided then that the time had come for the Great Escape I had been planning for months. I quickly grabbed our tote bags and began shoving them full of clothes, diapers, an old envelope full of money, and some food. It only took me twenty minutes or so to do as I had thought about it, and planned it out, as best as I could. I purposely left my cell phone on the table so it couldn't be traced. I knew he kept tabs on me. He'd trace it and find me before I could make it to the state line. Luckily, my car was an older model sedan and didn't have tracking capabilities like newer models had for roadside assistance or emergency aid. He had kept the new vehicle for himself—fully loaded, heated leather seats, a DVD player for our daughter to watch during trips... you get the picture.

My mind returned to our current predicament–traveling through a raging snowstorm on a quarter tank of gas in the middle of the night. I stifled a yawn and turned on the radio, quietly turning the dial to a local station. I didn't know where we were at this point— I had no phone, no GPS— just an old road atlas from 1998 that I had found shoved in an old box in the garage. Hopefully, there was a gas station or something up ahead.

A Garth Brooks song was playing on the radio and as it came to a halt, a news bulletin came across, the anchor's voice filling my car. "This just in. Due to a power outage from the current winter weather, the Pine Haven Correctional Center has announced that an inmate has escaped custody and is currently at large. Police from the tri-county area are currently looking for the man who was serving time for two counts of murder. The inmate, Jerod McKnight, stands 6 ft, 2 in, has brown eyes and a bald head. He has a large scar starting under his left eye down to his mouth. McKnight is considered to be most likely armed and dangerous. Do not approach him. Please call the state police as—"

I quickly turned the radio off. I did not need pictures of killers and police parading through my mind, adding to my stress. I glanced in my rearview mirror again sighing when I saw no headlights following us, just an empty highway covered in a thick layer of frozen precipitation.

A few miles down the road, as I was seriously starting to panic about the contents of my gas tank, I saw it. A low

building off the side of the road, nearly deserted looking
except for a couple of cars parked in the lot outside. A motel complete with a gas station. A sigh of relief escaped my
lips but as I slowed to turn into the parking lot, I realized
that the place was entirely dark, not a light anywhere. Shit.
Was it deserted or was the power just out due to all this
wind and snow?

I pulled into a space near the motel lobby's door and
turned off the engine. I debated whether I should wake
my daughter but decided I was too nervous to leave her
outside in this frozen mess. I got out, climbed in the back-
seat, gently removed her from her car seat, and approached
the motel lobby. The door easily opened with a dinging
sound overhead. The warm interior hugged my body as I
quickly looked around the darkened interior of the lobby,
deserted, yet lit by the light of an oil lamp on the counter.
Someone had to be here to light the lamp. I rang the bell
on the countertop, its ding sounding louder than normal
in the quiet, tomblike space. With a whisper of a sound
behind me, I turned to see a short man with a long beard
walking toward me.

"Sorry, but we are closed. Electricity's out due to the
storm," he said as he approached me. Then he seemed
to pause when he saw my daughter's feet sticking out

from under the blanket where she was sleeping against my shoulder.

"I just need some gas then. Am I able to at least do that?" I asked, trying not to let the panic into my voice. The man's face softened and he sighed.

"I'm sorry. The gas pumps run on electricity too."

"Oh...." I said, willing the tears of frustration and fear away. "Um...Well, how far is the next town? The next chance for gas?"

"About 20 miles up the road I'd say. But they are out of electricity too. Damn storm has most of the county under a blackout," the man said. "A whiteout and a blackout all in one night," he said with a chuckle.

"Look, I don't mean to be rude, but I really need to get some gas and get back on the road as soon as possible," I said, ignoring his joke. I wasn't in the mood.

"Well, I'd hate to see your little one caught out on the side of the road during a doozy like this. I'm not supposed to do this—liability and all—but I guess I can give you a room for tonight. Hopefully, the electric is back on in the morning and you can fill up and get on with your trip. How does that sound? The rooms are probably getting cold because the heat is out, but anything is better than sleeping in your car on a night like this."

"How much?" I asked, mentally calculating the amount of cash I had left.

"Ahh... I'll give it to you for free tonight out of inconvenience and lack of heat. The little one needs a good night's sleep," he said. "How old is she?"

"Eighteen months," I answered with relief. "And thank you for the room."

The bearded man smiled and handed me a key on an orange plastic keychain. The number 14 was scrawled messily on the back with a permanent marker. From under the cabinet, he produced a yellow battery-operated lantern.

"My name is Larry if you need anything. Just ring the bell here. Normally I'd say call from the room, but the phones are out too." he said with a shrug. I smiled and took the key and lantern from his outstretched hands. "Thanks. I'll see you tomorrow for gas...I hope." I said as I retreated outside.

A gust of arctic wind nearly bowed me over as I stepped outside and looked for our room. Luckily, Room 14 was near the end of the row, away from prying eyes. Hopefully, no one would remember us if Dean came around asking questions.

After I got my daughter into the hotel room, and nestled her into the bed, warm and safe, I locked her in and headed to move my car as quickly as possible. I pulled around to the side of the building and parked behind an old beat-up green metal dumpster. Hopefully, that would obscure my car from view until morning. Quickly grabbing our bags, I locked the car and headed toward the motel room door. I noticed a man walking across the parking lot towards the lobby. He nodded at me as I slid the key into my door. I quickly nodded back with a slight smile and went inside the room.

The motel room was like any other roadside inn across the country–grubby-looking carpet with mystery stains embedded in the fibers, and ugly bedspreads that always looked outdated no matter how new they were. The bathroom was surprisingly clean but dark in there so I couldn't be sure.

By lantern light, I tried to determine where we were by way of the outdated atlas. Based on road signage and Pinehaven Travel Plaza, I was fairly sure we were within a few miles of the state border. Not as much space between Dean and me as I had hoped but decent considering the snow. I'd have to get gas as soon as possible and get on the road at first light. I glanced at my watch–almost 1 a.m. I rubbed my eyes and changed into some warm sweatpants and a hoodie. Climbing into bed next to my daughter, I willed sleep to come but it didn't.

I must have dozed for a while because a noise outside my room suddenly startled me. I sat upright, quickly glancing around. My daughter was still sleeping next to me so I quietly climbed out of bed to investigate the source of the sound. Peeking through the miniblinds I could see someone walking around my car and looking into the dumpster. I tensed, the hair on the back of my neck standing on end, my breath coming in short, quick bursts. Was that him? Had he found me already? My stomach started to churn. A drop of sweat ran down my spine. I quickly looked around for a weapon— anything to ward him off. He would kill me if he found me.

While I continued to search for something–anything–in which to defend myself, there was a knock at the door. I whirled around, instantly on the defense. The knock came again, this time a little more urgent. I quietly crept up to the door to look out the peephole. Surely if it were Dean, he wouldn't knock and wait for an answer. He'd bust it down like he liked to do.

"Ma'am, it's Larry. From the front desk," came a muffled voice on the other side of the door. "Can you please open up? Something's happened."

A quick peek through the peephole confirmed it was Larry, the man from the front desk. I released the locks on the door and slowly opened it a crack. I was instantly smacked in the face by a brisk and bitter wind. I almost slammed the door shut by sheer reflex.

"What's wrong?" I asked, curious yet fearful. "What happened?"

"A man came here tonight after you arrived," Larry informed me. "He's wounded and I don't know what to do. Do you know anything about first aid? I'd call 911 but the landline is down and I don't have a cell phone."

"I...I don't know," I stammered. This was not what I was expecting. I thought for sure he was going to tell me.... No! Dean wasn't here. He couldn't be. I forced the thought from my head and looked at Larry. "I only know basic first-aid. Nothing fancy. I can have a look if you need though." I heard myself say. I was already regretting my decision to get involved but here I was.

I quickly gathered up my daughter, yet again, and followed Larry into another motel room a few doors down from mine. Two other people were standing inside the doorway wearing pajamas. Other motel guests I supposed. The man with the injury was lying on his back on the bed. His face was turned away from me but I was pretty sure it was the man I saw cutting across the parking lot. I approached the bed and looked down at him. He wore white tennis shoes and khaki pants much too thin for this weather. A small bloodstain seeped through his white tee shirt. I heard the man moan and my eyes quickly darted to his face. He then turned to me and I saw a long jagged line of puckered skin extending from under his left eye down to his mouth.

The escaped convict.

I swallowed hard and glanced at Larry and the other guests. Did they recognize the man? Had they heard the news alert? The convict— what was his name again? Oh yes!— Jerod McKnight grabbed at my hand when I looked back down at him. He appeared to have noticed my expression and quickening breath. He knew that I knew who he was.

"I can't help him. You're going to have to take him to the hospital," I said, backing away from the bed to get some distance between the child in my arms and the wounded murderer. The man tried to sit up just then, with a grunt, and reached out toward me again.

"Please, help me," he pleaded, holding his wound. The look in his eyes told me he wasn't as bad off as he was acting and that I didn't have a choice but to follow directions. Gulping down fear, I set my daughter down on the second bed, as far from the man as possible. She sat up, watching everything through sleepy, droopy eyes. I approached the man again, hesitantly, unsure how to escape this situation. I just wanted to leave, to take my daughter from this wretched room and get her to safety.

"Let me see your wound," I heard myself say. "I have no medical training, you know. Just some basic first aid classes from college."

I stood next to the bed, my legs bumping the mattress and ugly bedspread. I glanced up at the others in the room, nervous and jumpy. Larry handed me a flashlight, thick and sturdy, and I shone the light on the man lying on the bed. Jerod slowly pulled up his grubby, bloodstained shirt to reveal an abdomen covered in dark hairs and an intricate web of permanent pigment tattooing his flesh. A small round wound seemed to leak a trail of blood with every breath, every movement he made. I gulped. It looked like a gunshot wound, but being no doctor, I couldn't be sure. He had probably been shot while escaping tonight. I tried to school my expression and act like I knew what to do.

Feigning confidence, I informed Larry, "I'm going to need some supplies. Could you show me where the first aid kit is?" I was desperate to speak to Larry in private to devise a plan.

"Sure. At the front desk," Larry nodded, turning to leave the room. I grabbed my daughter and followed him outside into the blowing wind, snowflakes stinging my face. As we headed toward the motel's lobby, I heard someone come up behind me and turned to see the woman from the room following us. We all entered the lobby, slamming the door against the wind.

"Did you see that wound?" the woman asked in a hushed whisper, "Looks like a gunshot wound. Not that I'd know. I only watch television."

"Yes, I think it's a gunshot wound as well," I agreed, "I think he's Jerod McKnight, the escaped convict. I heard it on the news tonight."

Larry sucked in a breath, his eyes as large as saucers. The woman pulled out her cell phone and started dialing.

"Who are you calling?" I asked, irritated at the stress in my voice. I was sweating. We couldn't call the police. Not the police. Dean had probably already alerted them to my absence, my picture on every watchlist in the state. I felt panic rise like a geyser, threatening to make me vomit all over the worn rug on which I stood.

"The police," the woman stated, holding the phone to her ear. She turned away from me and started talking to someone on the other end of the line.

Shit! I had to get out of here. I had to run. Get my daughter to safety. I held the flashlight, the beam trembling in sync with my shaking hands.

As I turned to bolt, the woman's husband appeared at the lobby's door. He pushed in as I tried to leave. I could hear the trio talking about the situation, Larry sounding worried, but I didn't care. I ran as swiftly as I could over the slippery concrete of the sidewalk, the wind hitting me straight in the face. I felt my eyes sting as I pushed toward our room, where my car key and purse were still.

Suddenly, as I approached the inmate's door, an arm jutted out and grabbed me, pulling me into the depths of the room. The howling wind muffled my startled scream. As the door slammed shut behind us, my daughter and I found ourselves alone with Jerod McKnight, the escaped murderer.

"Leaving so soon?" he hissed in my ear. He grabbed the flashlight from my hand and shoved me towards the bed.

"I don't want any trouble. I want to leave," I pleaded with him. "I won't tell anyone I saw you here. Please."

"Shut up and sit down," Jerod hissed, nervously looking out of the broken blinds at the raging storm. I sat, huddled on the edge of the bed, frozen in fear, willing my brain to think of an escape plan.

A few moments later, as Jerod continued to look from me and then back outside, I still had come up with nothing. My brain wasn't helping me. I wanted to scream. I felt petrified in fear, but this situation was not nearly as dire as dealing with Dean. Unpredictable, hateful Dean.

Suddenly, the door flew open as though it had been kicked. Startled, Jerod and I jumped and turned to look at the open door hanging on its hinges. The police were here, crowded by Larry.

"Daddy!" my daughter squealed, reaching her chubby toddler arms out to the uniformed man glaring at me from across the room. My heart sank.

Dean had found us.

I felt like time was moving in slow motion. I heard Larry's comment on the impeccable response time from the police. I heard Dean tell Larry he'd take it from here and to go back to the office, his eyes never leaving mine. I felt frozen, incapable of moving, my breathing shallow and uneven. I knew his response time wasn't as on point as Larry thought. Dean had come after us, still wearing his uniform from work, and hadn't even stopped to change. Not that it would have mattered. He'd still flash his badge to get his way. He'd make me look crazy and then "arrest" me, taking me back to the hell house on Maple St where I'd been his prisoner for the past three years.

After watching Larry shuffle back toward the motel's lobby, Dean closed the door abruptly. "You bitch!" he seethed, apparently oblivious to the fact that an escaped convict was standing mere feet from him. Jerod stood still, flashlight in hand, and watched with a confused expression on his face, as Dean advanced toward me with rage-filled eyes.

The blow came, sudden and swift. I felt my body jolt as I slid off the bed, somehow still holding our daughter on my lap.

"You thought you could escape me? You could steal my kid?" Dean roared, lifting his hand to strike me again. "You actually thought I'd be too stupid to track you? God, what an idiot." He let out a humorless laugh and shook his head. "I've been tracking you since we were married. Haven't you ever looked under the bumper? Of course, you haven't. Well, let me enlighten you. I put a tracking device on your car when we returned from our honey-moon. No wife of mine was going to be parading around town, doing stuff that could soil my reputation," he spat. I froze, staring at some mysterious stain on the grubby carpet. "You can't escape me. You're mine. Forever and always." His hand raised higher to strike me again.

Suddenly, Dean stumbled backward, reaching for the desk to steady himself. Blood trickled down his face and again his body jolted.

It was only then that I saw Jerod, the escaped murderous convict, raise the flashlight a third time and ram it into Dean's skull. My husband fell, crumpled to the floor, as blood seeped into the carpet in an ever-widening pool. His body seemed to twitch a little and then remained still.

Eventually, I remembered to breathe. I gasped, taking in great gulps of air, my heart pounding out of my chest. My daughter squirmed lightly under the palm of my hand currently covering her face in an act of protection. I felt tears, sticky and hot, rolling down my face, as I watched Jerod leaning over Dean's limp form, checking for a pulse. Jerod turned to me then and nodded before standing back up. I continued to watch as he used his shirt to wipe down the handle of the flashlight to obliterate any fingerprints.

"You best get going," Jerod encouraged, not looking at me.

"But..." I stammered, unsure of what to say. This stranger, this convicted murderer, had just saved my child and me from a life full of pain, fear, and probable death.

"My daddy used to hit my mama and me," Jerod admitted, finally turning to look at me. "It ain't right. Go on now. Get the little girl away from here." The bald man with the gunshot wound gave me a slight smile. "I ain't getting outta here. The police will be here soon. I'm going back to prison. What's a few more years." he shrugged, thrusting his chin towards Dean's body.

"Thank you, Jerod," I whispered hoarsely, tears still rolling down my cheeks. I scooped my daughter up and ran from the room.

Within minutes, we were pulling out of the parking lot of that lonely roadside motel, the snow still swirling all around us. Up ahead, I saw blue and red lights flashing towards us. Seconds later, I could hear the sirens screaming as a line of police cruisers sped past us on the icy road. Keeping my speed steady, I continued traveling towards a new life, a happy life for my daughter and me. We never looked back again.

3

— • —

THE BLOODY BENDERS

Kansas, 1872

The beginning of my story, though a dark and horrible one, did not start as such. I was just a young man then, nearly eighteen when I set out looking for work. I never found myself useful behind a plow and wished to see bigger and greater things. I had heard of mountains so tall that the snow that fell upon them during the winter months never truly melted. I had heard stories of California and the gold there for the taking. Of the white-capped waves of the churning Pacific Ocean. I had heard of Indians on the Plains, hunting for buffalo with lances and arrows. I'd heard of eagles soaring over the prairie grasses looking for mice or other small game. It was so exciting to me that I found myself longing to go west, to see it all for myself and make my place in the world.

When I decided to head west and leave the Ohio farm where I had grown up, my family was disappointed. My

mother cried for three days straight and my father told me I
was an imbecile for even considering such an endeavor. He
ranted and raved about me leaving a "sure thing", his farm,
and venturing out on my own. That I had no idea of how
the world worked and that I'd be coming back home soon
enough, tail tucked between my legs. Now, before you pass
judgment on my father, please know that his stings and
barbs bounced off of me like rainwater on a newly oiled
tarp. I had been raised around such treatment and, though
I hated it, I was used to it. I wanted to get away from him
as much as I wanted to see the world.

Mind made up, I packed a few changes of clothes, a couple of books, some apples, and a loaf of bread my mother
had baked for me. I kissed her and sisters goodbye, and
with my meager life savings stashed deep in my sock, I
grabbed the handle of my suitcase and made my way to the
train station.

I had only traveled by train once before, to visit my Great
Nan in Pennsylvania before she died. It cost too much
for us to travel back then but I remember staring out the
windows and watching the cornfields roll past, the green
husks swaying and dancing in the wind. My sister, Betsy,
had to sit on my lap to look out of the window and I held
her there for hours while we counted sheep or cows to
pass the time. My mother, with a frown from my father,

bought us children a small tin of traveling treats, which we shared with delight. Father refused to partake, claiming them a "wretched waste of hard-earned money." We three children ate the sweets in silence, avoiding our father's dour gaze yet slipping small smiles at Mother when she dared to make eye contact with us. My poor sister, Amelia, accidentally dropped a treat onto the floor of the train car and we watched it roll over to Father's shoe, our breaths stuck in our throats. I remember Amelia crying softly to herself after that, holding her reddened cheek after Father had struck her for her carelessness. It was then that I began to truly hate my father. I vowed then that I would never be like him.

Now, since leaving Ohio by train, I had struck up various deals with fellow travelers to make my way westward. My meager funds were quickly depleting and I soon found myself in want of employment as I needed to eat and sleep somewhere. On warmer, dry nights, I often found places outdoors to sleep, usually in fields or along some lonely road. I remember laying there on my back, staring up at the stars, wondering how Betsy and Amelia were faring with me gone. I wondered if Father would turn his aggression on them and I felt shame. Part of me wished I had never left them with him, as he was a hateful and vengeful person.

But the other part of me knew I needed to get away and become my own man.

It was during my search for employment when I happened upon a small tavern on the Kansas/Missouri border one rainy night in mid-June. I was on foot, as I had no other means of transportation when the sky turned charcoal and the heavens opened in a deluge like none other. I ran with haste to the nearest building even as the night sky lit with lightning and the deafening rumbles of thunder shook the panes of glass in the windows. Standing in the tavern doorway, looking quite sodden, I slowly caught my breath whilst looking around at my surroundings.

The tavern, a small dining room with a bar, was half full with men laughing, drinking, and playing cards. A few women, though not ladies surely, sat around near the men, talking in low tones and showing too much skin for mixed company. Feeling awkward, my face suddenly heated, I lowered my gaze and slid into the booth nearest the door. Water dripped from the hem of my trousers and I knew I was leaving mud on the floor under my feet, but I didn't, couldn't, ask for a towel.

"What'll be?" came a gruff voice above me. With a glance up I noticed the barman standing over me expectantly.

"Just some water, please," I said, even as my stomach began to grumble. It had been since morning that I had last eaten and the scent of food wafting from the kitchen now assaulted my nostrils. Quickly thinking about how much money I had left, I hastily added, "And maybe some stew or a sandwich if you have it." With a nod, the barman left me alone.

I was tired from my day, walking westward for most of it. I had a small respite when I had offered to help load a wagon laden with crates of apples in exchange for a ride to the nearest town. The ride had been bumpy but enjoyable, the apple man talkative and animated. Once in the town, I helped unload the wagon and the man had given me a small burlap sack of apples. I would savor them as they would be my only food now until I could procure another source of income.

That is, until the stew that was suddenly put before me. The barman had returned and had set a small crock full of steaming meat stew, laden with barley and vegetables. The scent instantly caused my mouth to water and I thanked the man. With a nod, the barman set a hunk of fresh bread on the table next to my bowl of stew. As he stepped away, I picked up the spoon and dug into my feast. It was quite possibly the best stew I had ever eaten but maybe I thought that because I was so hungry.

So enthralled with my meal, that I almost missed hearing the front door open to reveal the storm raging outside.

Enter Mr. Barnaby William Plythe, although, at that moment, I had no idea what his name was.

The man stood in the doorway, taking a perusal of his surroundings before slowly walking towards me and taking a seat at a table nearby. The man's clothing and general persona spoke of wealth and as he sat down, many of the other patrons stopped the camaraderie to stare. The man simply ignored them. I watched as he reached into his coat pocket, pulled out a piece of correspondence of some kind, and began to read.

I continued to watch quietly from my booth, slowly sipping and savoring my feast, as the barman came forward to speak to the newcomer. I listened as the man ordered a steak dinner, with mashed potatoes 'but hold the parsley' and a serving of sweetened carrots. As the barman took the order and walked away, the man turned and looked directly at me. Caught staring, I quickly looked down and stirred my spoon in the now-empty crock. Wishing the man would stop his perusal, as it unnerved me greatly, I feigned searching for something in my pocket, anything but staring back at him.

When I glanced up, he was standing at my table, still watching me curiously. I slowly looked up into his face, his blue eyes catching my every move.

"Excuse me," he finally said, "I don't mean to bother you but are you Alfred Banockburn, perchance?"

"No, sir," I answered, somewhat confused at his inquiry. "My name is Charlie. I don't know anyone by that name."

"No mind," the man replied, taking a seat across from me, uninvited yet not unwelcome. "My name is Barnaby William Plythe. I was to meet Mr. Banockburn here to interview for a job." I said nothing, merely sat there chewing on the last of my bread.

"I should give him a few minutes, but truly, I just want to get on with my night," Plythe stated, suddenly seeming tired. He sighed heavily and looked over his shoulder towards the kitchen.

"What kind of job is he interviewing for?" I asked finally, trying to break the silence spreading between this strange man and myself.

"A valet. A traveling companion of sorts," Plythe explained, looking back at me. "I am traveling west and need companionship and someone to drive me, watch my luggage, take care of lodging, meals. I can't be bothered by it all and going alone sounds lonesome."

My pulse quickened. Could this be my chance? To travel west and make something of myself? Now, I was only a farm boy from Ohio and knew nothing of being a valet but I was smart, a quick learner to be sure.

"Well, Mr. Plythe," I heard myself say, "I just so happen to be looking for employment to make my way out west. Perhaps I could interview for the job, sir."

Barnaby William Plythe leaned back in the seat then, eyeing my person with interest. After a moment of scrutiny, he asked, "Have you ever served as a valet before?"

"No, sir, but I am a quick study and I need a job," I said quickly, unsure of how hard the job could be. The barman came just then and set Plythe's food in front of him and the man dug in. He chewed for a few moments, watching me all the while. He swallowed then and took a drink of his cider.

"I'm sure you could," he finally said, dabbing at the corners of his mouth with his linen napkin. "Do you live around here?"

"No, sir," I offered. "I am from Ohio and only arrived in Kansas today. I have been traveling and working odd jobs along the way. My goal is to reach California, see the ocean, and explore the country along the way."

"And what will you do then? After you see the ocean?" Plythe asked, taking another bite of his steak.

"I guess I will just keep exploring. See where the road takes me," I admitted, feeling slightly foolish for not having a plan after seeing the mighty Pacific.

Plythe grinned at me then. "Sounds like a wonderful adventure, young man! It looks like Mr. Banockburn is out of luck. I think you and I would make a good team if you are interested in joining me."

What luck! I smiled at him and nodded. "Why, Mr. Plythe, I do believe this is an answer to my prayers! When do we leave?"

***

Over the next week or so, Mr. Plythe and I set about getting supplies in order and procuring a wagon and two horses. He paid for it all with cash as though it cost nothing and I wondered what it must be like to never worry about how much something cost. I was given a new three-piece black suit, a pair of shiny black leather shoes, a sharp Derby hat, and an extra white cotton shirt and dark gray trousers. Mr. Plythe assured me that I was a new man and should rid myself of the past, suggesting I burn my old clothes as a symbol of moving forward. He then added that they also stunk and he didn't want to smell them all the way to California. Though at first hurt, I agreed. They did stink.

Finally, our day of departure arrived, sunny and balmy. I was both excited and apprehensive as Mr. Plythe, though friendly, was still very much a stranger to me. He was, however, my employer, and my only foreseeable way to California. With a quick shake of the reins, we were off, sitting side by side on the wagon seat as we jostled out of town.

The road before us, known as the Great Osage Trail, was the only real roadway of sorts out west through Kansas in those days. Traveled by various types of people and beast alike, the roadway was heavily populated close to town but as we slowly made our progression towards the western horizon, the travelers thinned out. Before long, Plythe and I were by ourselves with nothing but the rolling horizon and the rumps of the horses to look at.

Conversation flowed between the two of us easily and I soon learned that Mr. Plythe was forty-three, never married, and had originated from Boston, the son of a prestigious lawyer. He'd followed his father's footsteps and had also become a lawyer, intending to start a law practice of his own once he made it to California. He told me about his sweetheart, Molly, who had broken his heart and married someone else, and about his old dog, Reb, who'd died when he was a boy of twelve.

I told Plythe about growing up on a farm in rural Ohio, about my two sisters, Betsy and Amelia, and about my dog, Warden, who'd been run over by a milk truck on my tenth birthday. Father had told me not to cry over a dog as it showed a weakness of personality and mind. My mother, however, had held me while I sobbed once Father had gone back to the field. Poor Mother.

I wondered about her now, as I sat next to my new employer, reigns in my hands, as we slowly made our way west. I hoped she was well and that Father hadn't finally broken her spirit. I vowed then, sitting in that jostling wagon, to write to my mother as soon as I could to tell her about my new employment.

We had been traveling for four days, camping out in a canvas tent each night and cooking over a campfire. I had, up until then, never cooked, much less over a fire, but together, Plythe and I made do. We talked about eating a nice warm meal at a real table and sleeping in a real bed again someday. We would laugh and daydream as we slowly lumbered on through the flat terrain.

One day, a few days into our journey, we passed a cross-road with some road signs and a notice board near the roadway. A few houses could be seen a far distance off but it was a sign on the notice board that caught our eye. "Bender Inn, warm meals and beds for reasonable rates, 2 miles west," the sign read. Another one advertised a farm for sale, one for a plow.

"Oh, this could be fun." Plythe grinned, pointing to another flyer with a crude drawing on a crystal ball. "Need spiritual guidance? Need to know your future? Inquire at Bender Inn," he read.

"A fortune teller?" I asked, unsure if I even believed in such nonsense.

"Why yes!" Plythe exclaimed, slapping me on the back. "I hear it's just for fun but if you're scared....."

"I'm not scared," I assured him, a little too hastily. It wasn't that I was afraid. I just didn't know if I wanted to know what the future had in store for me.

Looking back now, I wish I had been scared. I wish I had known what the future held for us. If I had, I never would have gone to the Bender Inn.

***

We arrived at Bender Inn when the sun was starting to dip low in the sky. As we pulled the wagon off of the road and onto the bumpy, rocky trail to the inn, I looked around at the small building before us. It was not much of an inn, as far as Eastern standards went, but out here on the Kansas plains I supposed it was adequate.

The small rectangular cabin sat situated on a relatively flat, treeless piece of land. Behind the small dwelling, I could see a barn and some horses peering out at us as we approached. A large vegetable garden grew near the house.

As we drew nearer I could see a few red tomatoes weighing down the vines. Ears of corn grew from tall, lush stalks near the garden. And the sweet peas! Never had I seen sweet peas growing so plentiful in such a dry and desolate place. I wondered what their secret was, as I had never had such a green thumb. Mother had been the one to make our kitchen garden thrive back home. I tried to help but everything I planted would just wither and die.

Beyond the barn, I could see a small orchard, full of young apple and peach trees. Mr. Plythe had been paying me a small wage, along with food and board, for my services and I vowed then that I would inquire about purchasing some apples for our journey westward.

As we pulled up in front of the small house, a young woman and old man came out and began walking towards us. Mr. Plythe waved at them in greeting and the woman just gave a nod in response. The old man said nothing, a slight scowl on his face.

"Greetings!" Mr. Plythe called as I hopped down from the wagon quickly to place his small step stool beneath his feet. He had told me on the first day of my employment that I was to do this so that he wouldn't strain his back in any way as he disembarked. Though I hardly thought he'd strain himself, I remained quiet and obliged him.

"Hello. What can we do for you tonight?" the woman asked, looking up at me with a small smile on her lips. I said nothing, waiting for Mr. Plythe to take the lead as I was just the valet.

"I will be needing a hot meal, and lodgings for tonight if you have it," Plythe explained, smiling at the grumpy old man and the younger woman standing in front of us.

"Certainly, sir," the young woman nodded. The old man finally spoke, speaking in low, guttural sounds. German from the sounds of it. The woman nodded to him and the old man went back into the house.

"Do you need a meal too?" she asked me, a strange smile crossing her face.

"Yes, ma'am," I nodded as I began gathering up the reins. "Where would you like for me to bed the horses tonight?"

"The barn will do," the woman gestured towards the barn near the rear of the house. She turned back to Mr. Plythe, "My name is Kate Bender. That was Pa."

"I'm Barnaby William Plythe, from Boston," Plythe announced, with a slight puff of his chest. "This is Charlie, my valet. He will bed with the horses and take his meal in the barn."

I turned and looked at Plythe, unsure why he was suddenly acting so distant. Yes, I was in his employ but until now, he had treated me as an equal for the most part and had been friendly. It was then that I saw the rapacious glint in his eye as he spoke to Kate Bender, eyeing her womanly form openly. She seemed to notice his attention and smiled up at him.

"This way then, sir," she instructed, "Ma is almost done cooking dinner." She turned to me then and commanded, "Charlie, go ahead and unhitch the horses, put them to pasture. My brother, John, should be out there now and will help you feed them. I'll be out shortly with your meal." And with that, she and Plythe slowly made their way towards the small cabin.

The barn's interior was dark when I approached and I wondered where her brother was. I pulled the wagon up outside the paddock fence and went about unhitching the two horses when a man, a few years older than myself, came out from the gloomy interior of the barn. He smiled when he saw me, courteously enough, and began walking towards the Plythe wagon.

"Hello! It's looking to be a nice night tonight, isn't it?" he greeted me with a goofy grin on his face. I nodded and looked towards the setting sun, the sky an array of pinks and violets. The man let out a small giggle and pointed to some birds flying around the barn's roof.

"Them ain't birds. Them's bats," he said, pointing. "They eat the skeeters." Suddenly, he slapped at his arm as though killing a mosquito, and then erupted in laughter. "He's dead now."

It didn't take long for me to realize that poor John was a little slow. He kept laughing and giggling at things that were not amusing. I humored him and talked about bats and mosquitoes as I unhitched the horses and put them to pasture. After a few minutes of John talking incessantly, I saw Kate making her way towards me from the house, carrying a tray of food.

"John, Pa needs you in the house now," Kate said, stopping in front of me but looking at her brother. "Go on now. I'll help Charlie get settled in." John nodded and with a huge grin and an eerie giggle, he bounded toward the house. Kate and I watched him go and then she turned to me. "There are blankets in the trunk by the tack room. Here, I'll show you."

I followed her into the darkened barn where she set the tray of food down on an upturned barrel. Looking around, I noticed two wagons parked inside, a few saddles strewn about, and the trunk Kate had mentioned. She stopped in front of the steamer trunk and bent to open it, revealing the contents. It was packed full of various blankets and quilts. She grabbed two or three from the top of the pile and brought them over toward a stack of straw bales that stretched almost to the barn's eaves.

"You'll sleep here tonight," she instructed, as though the topic was not up for discussion. I simply nodded, taking the blankets from her and setting about making a bed of sorts on the bales of straw.

"You wanna touch it?" she asked, looking up at me, questioningly. Confused, I shook my head.

"Touch what?" I asked, looking around my feet, unsure what she was talking about. And then to my utter embarrassment, Kate pulled the hem of her dress up past her knees, flashing way too much skin for a decent conversation. I could feel my face heating up, my palms sweaty. I instantly dropped my gaze and turned away, pouring all my energy into making myself a bed.

Kate laughed then, dropped her hem back, and put her hands on her hips. "My, my, but you *are* different," she commented. "Most gents take me up on my offer. I don't know why you're so red." She started laughing again and went to get my food off of the barrel.

"I'm just being a gentleman, ma'am," I muttered with a thanks for the food. I sat down on a bale of straw and just stared at my food for the longest time.

"Well, gentleman or not, it isn't a big deal," Kate sighed, sitting down on another bale of straw a few feet away. "I think it's perfectly normal to be with whoever you want, whenever you want. Society puts irrational constraints on people. Why do you think everyone is so crazy these days?" She plucked at some loose straw and flung it away from her.

"I'm just waiting until I meet the right girl. That's all," I explained, still not making eye contact. I'd only just met this woman and already she felt emboldened to speak on such topics with a stranger! I felt my pulse increase further as my face continued to flush.

"I like you, Charlie," Kate said then, looking at me. "You're different. Can I do something for you?" Apprehensive, I gave her a look and she laughed quietly. "Not that, silly. Here, give me your hands."

I slowly put my bread down and held out my hands. She took them in her own hands, calloused and warm, and closed her eyes.

At first, I was confused at what she was doing, and right when I was about to ask, her eyes opened and she stared into mine.

"Leave this place," she whispered urgently. "Leave now, Charlie, and don't look back."

"Leave? But we've only just gotten here and I'm so tired," I asked, my mind spinning. "Why must I leave? And what about Mr. Plythe?"

"It's not safe here for you, Charlie. They will come," she leaned into me with a harsh whisper.

"Who? Who will come?" I asked as she stood and slowly tried to pull me up.

"Them. Go while you still can." With that, she began tugging at my hands, pulling me towards the front of the barn.

"But what about Mr. Plythe?" I asked, as I slowly came to a halt next to a parked wagon in the barn. "He's my employer and I am to care for his needs."

"Soon, you will be looking for a new employer," Kate sighed, starting to look a little exasperated. "He is nothing to you. Leave, Charlie!" It was then that John came out of the house and called for Kate, saying something about doing a reading for Mr. Plythe.

She gave me a look, her eyes serious, her mouth set in a grim line. "I tried to warn you, dear boy. I tried," she whispered gravely as she turned to head toward the house where John was waiting.

I sat there, alone in the barn, for a few moments contemplating what she had said and what I should do. Never one to be an alarmist, I was afraid to cause drama and go get Mr. Plythe. Kate had made it seem as though he were in danger somehow.

The sun had all but set by now, the farmyard enshrouded with deep shadows. I decided to quietly sneak up to the small inn and check it out for myself. The inn, nothing more than a small rectangular cabin with a few windows, sat a few hundred yards away from the barn.

Keeping to the shadows, I quietly slunk up to the back wall before stopping to listen. I could hear voices coming from within but couldn't decipher what was being said. Slowly, I crept up to the nearest window and cautiously took a peek inside. The window was open a few inches, giving me a good view of the inside of the inn.

The house seemed to be divided into two parts. One appeared to serve as the diner turned general store. A few shelves lined the walls, holding tins of food and canned vegetables. Smoked meat hung from the beams and a large cast iron cook stove sat in the corner. An older woman with a deeply lined scowl on her face moved about the room, from stove to table, and back again. A small table sat in the middle of the room, a dark cloth covering it. At the table sat Kate, a jeweled necklace and shawl draped over her head. Her eyes were closed and she seemed to be humming or moaning deep in her throat as she rolled her head from side to side as if in a trance.

Mr. Plythe sat across from her at the table, his back against what looked to be a large piece of canvas, or perhaps a wagon cover, that served as a room divider. I could only speculate that their living quarters were on the other side of the hanging curtain. Mr. Plythe sat, holding Kate's hands and staring at her with lust-filled eyes. Seeing Mr. Plythe like that made me begin to question my good opinion of him.

John came around the house then, almost to where I was standing, but walked on. Thankfully I was deep enough in the shadows to go undetected. I watched as he went in the front door, whispered something to the older woman at the stove, and then slipped behind the curtain. Almost instantaneously, Kate's moans and head weaves increased as her grip on Plythe's hands appeared to tighten. Plythe licked his lips excitedly, leaning into the table just a bit, waiting to hear about Kate's vision for his future.

Suddenly, and without warning, an axe blow came from behind the curtain straight into the back of Mr. Plythe's head. I stifled a gasp of horror as the scene unfolded before me. Mr. Plythe's body listed to the side, convulsing as blood poured out of his decimated skull. Eventually, the poor man fell off the chair, and landed with a thud, all the while gasping and twitching. It was then that John grabbed a knife from the dining table and in one swift motion, slashed my employer's throat, severing great vessels and tendons along the way. I felt bile rise in my throat and quickly put my hand over my gaping mouth to keep my wails from escaping along with my dinner. I began to sweat, my heart racing. I must run! But run where? This devil's land was flat and open for miles in all directions. Surely they would see me make my escape. I continued to watch as Kate and Pa grabbed Mr. Plythe's feet and slowly dragged him behind the curtain, to do what, I didn't know. My mind screamed for me to run, to grab a horse, and leave this place.

It hit me then. They knew I was here. Kate herself had told me to leave, that I was in danger of them. Surely they would come for me next! With haste and a prayer in my heart, I ran as quickly as I could across the uneven ground, hoping I didn't step into a hole in the dark. Not even bothering to saddle a horse, I quickly hopped the rickety corral fence and approached one of Mr. Plythe's horses. The horse nickered at me as I came close, sidestepping some until he realized it was me. I quickly felt for the harness and pulled the horse towards the small barn, even as I heard the front door of the house open. They were coming! Never in all my days growing up on that farm in Ohio have I ever given a horse the bit and buckled a bridle so fast. My hands were shaking as I quickly hopped up on a bail of straw, mounted the tall saddle-less gelding, and made my way out the back of the barn. I could hear the Benders opening the barn door looking for me even as I heeled the gelding into a gallop. Away from that horrible place.

Away from Hell.

I have never spoken of that day. Until now. It will forever be etched in my brain, causing me many a sleepless night. It wasn't until a few months after that fateful night that I saw a newspaper article from back East. The paper was three weeks old at the time, rumpled and stained with coffee or some such but it was the front page headline that caught my eye. "The Bloody Benders: Killer Family Slays at Least a Dozen" was splashed across the front page and under the headline, a photo of that hideous inn.

I grabbed the paper with shaking hands and slowly sunk to my seat in a little cafe just outside of Lincoln. Spreading the battered paper as flat as I could, I began to read. According to the newsprint, a search party looking for a missing doctor had arrived at the Bender Inn only to find it deserted, the animals half-starved. Upon entering the dwelling, the stench of death and rot assaulted the men so fiercely that they could hardly enter the home, but when they did they found the odor to be coming from a trap door in the floor, beneath the bed. There, in the bottom of the pit, was so much blood, clotted and lumpy, that it had soaked into the soil nearly half a foot deep. The search party eventually moved the entire structure looking for human remains but found nothing under the house.

It wasn't until they searched the garden and apple orchard that they found multiple remains with their skulls shattered and throats slit. Only the doctor's body was ever claimed. The law surmised that the family came from behind the curtain with an axe and knife, slaughtered the travelers, and then stored their bodies in the pit until they could strip them of their valuables and dump their remains in the garden. With a rueful smile, I guess I had found the secret to their green thumbs. I wondered if Mr. Plythe's family ever claimed his body, or if he was ever even identified. Part of me felt as though I should go back to Kansas and tell the sheriff what I had witnessed, but what would that do? The family was long gone at this point and if I was being honest with myself, I was just too scared to return there.

After paying for my coffee and stew, I left the cafe with a slight wave and a smile to the woman behind the counter. Stepping out onto the boardwalk, I folded the newspaper roughly and shoved it in the nearest trash bin. As I approached the post office, I pulled out a letter to my dear mother in Ohio, gave it to the clerk, and left Lincoln, never to look back.

Author's Note: The previous story is a work of fiction based on true-life events that occurred in Kansas in the 1870s. The Benders and their crimes as America's first known serial killer family will always be part of the darker side of our history. As in this story, the real-life family were never caught although some people reported sightings of them from time to time. None of the claims could be substantiated and the mystery surrounding their whereabouts remains.

4

THE AXE MAN OF TATE FARM

Everyone around here knows of the Tate Farm Slayings. It happened way before our time, but we all know the story, at least our version of it. I honestly don't know the facts, of course, because I wasn't there, but the way I heard it, it was a nightmare.

Now, I don't believe in ghosts. Let me just say that from the beginning. I'm not a believer in the supernatural or any of that hocus pocus bullshit. It's pure nonsense if you ask me. I've been a skeptic of the Tate story for as long as I can remember.

Or at least I was.

According to old newspaper clippings and word of mouth, the Tate Farm Slayings, as they've been called, happened one humid night in July way back in 1892. As the story goes, Thaddeus Tate, the owner of the farm, had gone crazy one night and hacked his entire family to bits with the axe he usually used for chopping wood. Locals reported back then that Tate had seemed normal, acting like his usual self, and then, out of nowhere, slaughtered his family.

Throughout the generations, the motive has morphed into one of mental illness, perhaps a drunken rage, or the best one yet, ghosts or demons from the nether-world. Now, like I said, I think the netherworld option is hogwash. Old Mr. Tate probably just got tired of the day-to-day monotony of old-time farm life and just went crazy. At least that's my guess.

Ever since that hideous night in 1892, the old white farmhouse at the edge of town has sat empty for the most part. There have been a few families that have moved in but they only stay for a few weeks at a time, six months tops. Nobody knows what happened to them all. They kind of just vanished in the night, moved on, and never came back.

The murders of that night are not the only deaths that the old house has seen. Since the Tate slayings, three other people have been killed in that house, all involving an axe. Now, you're probably wondering what kind of yarn I'm spinning, but let me tell you, it's God's honest truth.

You see, my name is Matthew Tate, and old man Thaddeus was my great, great, great uncle. That old two-storied farmhouse with the veranda and peeling white paint has been in our family for generations. Now, I've never been inside of it, only walked around outside, but I can feel a darkness there. Like I said before, I don't believe in ghosts, demons, spirits, whatever. I just get a heavy feeling there. There has been so much death and violence, that it's easy to see why.

About a decade or so after old man Tate slaughtered his family, another family member moved into the house. They lasted all of three weeks and then moved back to Pennsylvania or wherever it was they were from. To this day, no one knows for sure what happened. I have heard claims of ghostly activity making them leave but I think that's ridiculous. Surely there is a better explanation.

Again, that old house sat empty, dark, and lonely for another twenty years or so. This time, it was 1932, and my great-great-grandfather, Angus Tate, moved his family in. From what I've read, his family was larger and they had outgrown their previous home. The empty farmhouse, land, and outbuildings sounded like a good opportunity for them to start a new life. The entire country struggled through the Great Depression and times were hard. With multiple children to feed, Angus Tate quickly went to work, plowing and turning the fallow ground into something worthwhile.

They had been living in the old house for a few months and everything seemed to be going well. The crops were growing, and the animals thriving. Then one evening, while the older children were at a midsummer get-together at a neighboring farm, something horrible happened. Local newspapers claim that Angus Tate took the axe from his woodpile, drugged it inside of the house, and after climbing the stairs to the second floor, he axed his wife and two youngest children to death in their sleep. Reporters claimed that the walls were painted red with blood, and the bodies mutilated almost beyond recognition. It was a neighbor who, when bringing the older Tate children home from the party, had found the bodies of the victims. Angus Tate, who had slit his own wrists, bled out next to his murdered wife. To this day, no one knows why Angus would have done something so hideous, so depraved.

Since that night in 1932, there have been a few tenants who've lived there for short periods but no other violence that I have heard of. The last tenant moved out years ago and the house, once again, sat empty. The older, remaining Tate children went to live with distant relatives in a neighboring state.

Now, all those years after the last Tates were viciously slain by their patriarch, I was the next family member to move in.

I had recently married my longtime girlfriend, Maggie. She is in real estate and loves old houses so when I showed her the old family farmhouse she was overcome with excitement. After a few weeks of her begging to move in and remodel it, leaving our two-bedroom apartment in the city, I finally caved. Anything to make her happy. I had told her about the deaths but left out most of the gory details. Like I said before, I was sure that the truth had been embellished for the benefit of a good story.

Now, as I pulled the moving truck up the overgrown driveway leading to the house, I looked around at all the work that needed to be done and silently wondered what kind of mess I had gotten myself into.

"There it is!" Maggie exclaimed when the house came into view. The look on her face was one of sheer delight. I smiled at her as we continued up the driveway. As I parked and turned off the ignition, she was out of the truck before I even had my seat belt off.

"Matt! Check out that veranda! We could put some porch swings up!" Maggie exclaimed, running around like a kid in a candy store.

"Okay, Mags, whatever you want," I smiled, watching her take in our new home for the first time. "Just watch out for snakes," I added, nodding toward the overgrown yard. No one had been here for quite some time, except for some lowlife who had painted a neon pink phallic symbol on the front door. The door hung open, kicked in years ago from the looks of it. Most of the windows were still boarded up. Those that weren't were broken or cracked.

"You sure about this, Maggie? It's kind of a mess," I questioned her again for what felt like the twelfth time, walking around the front yard, looking at the overgrown flower gardens. A few moments later, I approached the house, taking gingerly steps across the planked floor of the veranda. The porches' floor felt firm underfoot, somewhat surprising me. I was half expecting my foot would go through the old wood and get caught.

"Oh! Check this out!" I heard my wife call from inside the house. I followed the sound of her voice, slowly stepping into the dimmed interior for the first time in my life. I instantly felt the dark foreboding I had felt outside on earlier occasions. Not a scary feeling, or one of imminent doom, but rather a heavy oppression, almost as though the house itself was filled with a deep sorrow from all that it had witnessed.

Directly in front of me stood a tall stairway leading up to the upper floors. Dust bunnies, piles of leaves, mouse droppings, and even a used condom, scattered the entryway floor. Peeling yellowed wallpaper, once a light green color with a light vine pattern throughout, covered the walls. Past the stairway, through the murky darkness, I could make out two doorways leading to rooms in the rear of the house. To my left appeared to be the sitting room, once beautiful I'm sure. It now appeared damp and moldy, with cobwebs hanging from the ceiling and across the mantle. Wires stuck out of a hole in the ceiling where a light fixture had once been. An old couch sat upturned in the middle of the room, stuffing erupting from rents in the fabric. From the mouse droppings around the couch, it was evident they were the culprits.

"Matt, are you coming?" I heard Maggie call again, her voice traveling from the area opposite the sitting room. I quickly passed through the entryway again and into the old dining room. Maggie stood near the fireplace, holding an old book, dusty and yellowed with age.

"Check this out. I found it in the wall." Maggie said, handing me the book and then dusting her hands off on her shorts.

"*In* the wall?" I asked, wiping the dust from the cover and turning the book over in my hands.

"Yeah. I accidentally kicked the baseboard over there by the mantle. A piece fell loose and I saw the book sticking out." Maggie shrugged, apparently already bored with the book, as she moved on toward the sitting room. I walked to the open front door and used the sunlight pouring through it to study the book.

It appeared to be an old diary, kept hidden all these years. The book was full of handwritten entries, even a few drawings of various animals and flowers. Each page was signed "S.T." and the dates at the top of the entries, smudged from age, were dated as far back as 1891. This had to belong to one of the original Tates, all those years ago, but I didn't know all the children's names. I knew Thadeus's wife's name was Elizabeth, but the children's names were unknown to me. I made a mental note to research the original family and read the diary, but for now, I decided to continue exploring the house.

As expected, the rest of the house was in just as bad condition upstairs as it was downstairs. There were four large bedrooms upstairs and a bathroom that had been converted from a large closet. Because some of the windows were still boarded up, the interior was dark and murky. Spiders and other small creatures scurried deeper into the shadows as I entered each room. From the looks of it, the roof seemed to be in decent condition, although I would have someone come out and confirm. When I walked into the bedroom to the left of the staircase, toward the back of the house, I felt an instant unease.

My pulse suddenly elevated and I had a deep desire to run from the room. To be anywhere but there. I didn't know what triggered the feeling at first, and then I realized. I was standing in the same bedroom where the original Tate children had been slain, and then, decades later, where two more had met the same grisly fate. I felt numb like I was paralyzed and couldn't move, as though all the air had been sucked out of the room. My eyes roamed over the wooden rocking horse, covered in cobwebs, in the corner of the room. I noticed some small flowers that appeared to be hand-painted on the wall near an old metal bed frame, rusted with age. I felt like vomiting when I noticed something on the floor near the bed. A dark stain of some sort. It appeared someone had tried to scrub it out at some point in time, but I knew what it was. Blood.

Suddenly, I felt a light pressure on my shoulder, and I jumped. Whipping around, I found Maggie standing there, her hand still raised from where she'd set it on my shoulder.

"Whoa, big guy! You see a ghost or something?" she teased, looking at me with concern in her eyes. "You seem jumpy." When I didn't say anything, she asked, "I called for you. Didn't you hear me?"

"No. Let's just go back downstairs." I mumbled, pushing past her and heading for the stairs. I headed straight outside, into the sun, taking a big breath and trying to shake the feeling of unease.

We poked around in the outbuildings and fallow fields after that, taking our time exploring. The old barn would probably need to be demolished as it had settled over time and now leaned precariously, the boards rotten in places. The old foundation, moldering with age, didn't look to be in much better condition. So much work to be done, but where to start? Had I gotten us into a bad situation? Maggie, of course, only saw the goodness of the place, the potential. I, however, only saw the darkness. I knew what had happened all those years ago from family stories being passed down from generation to generation. I'd told Maggie that there had been a death in the house but hadn't elaborated. I hadn't shared my personal opinion that both Angus and his predecessor, Thaddeus, had to have had some kind of mental illness or something. Why else would they murder their families in their sleep? Yeah, I was their descendant, but I did not believe they were following the commands of some witch demon or whatever crazy theories people had come up with. There was no Tate family curse. There had to be a simple, logical explanation.

***

Over the next few days, we worked hard cleaning out the old house so that we could begin restoring it. We'd been staying at a small hotel in town but spent our days removing trash and leaves from the interior and veranda. We pulled weeds, and I mowed what I could. The inside of the house had slowly begun taking shape, too. What little furniture we owned had been stored in the sitting room downstairs those first few days, but before long we had moved it into the appropriate rooms. With a little hard work, we were able to salvage the antique dining table and chairs, although they would need to be reupholstered. Unfortunately, the settee and chair in the sitting room were complete losses due to the mice nests in them.

During our first evening after officially moving in, a storm rolled through with lightning flashing and thunder shaking the house. Despite the weather, we had an easy meal of instant mashed potatoes and Polish kielbasa cooked to perfection on our propane camp stove. Maggie, always the joker, wore her white apron and flipped the frying meat with gusto as though she were a top chef at a ritzy restaurant. Until the new stove got delivered next week, she'd be the Queen of the Propane Camp Stove.

"Thank you, honey," I smiled appreciatively at her while picking up our paper plates and plastic cutlery and disposing of them in the trash can. Our real plates and silverware were still packed in boxes stacked in the corner of the old kitchen. "That was pretty good!"

"Glad you liked it. I worked *so* hard on it!" Maggie laughed, a twinkle in her eye. "Wine?" she asked, pulling a bottle of wine out of the ice-packed cooler.

"Nah, none for me. Thanks though," I said, cleaning up the rest of the dinner mess. I was exhausted from the day and, if we were fully moved in, I'd be headed to my chair to watch random cable shows until I fell asleep. I yawned now at the thought. No cable for us until it got hooked up, and besides, the television was still wrapped up in bubble wrap and moving blankets.

"Tired so soon?" Maggie asked, coming to me and wrapping her arms around my neck. I leaned in and kissed her lightly on the lips and she smiled.

"Yes. I'm exhausted. Where are the bed linens?" I asked, looking into her blue eyes. "Do we even know?"

"Upstairs. I took them up there myself earlier," Maggie said proudly. Then her face changed into a mischievous grin. "Maybe I should help you put them on the bed?" she added, giving me a quick yet seductive kiss before racing for the stairs.

I ran after her, laughing and tripping up the stairs. She wasn't at the top of the stairs though, and the hallway was dark. "Where'd you go?" I called into the shadows. I paused to listen but heard nothing over the rain pelting the windows and my ragged breathing. "Mags?" I called again, but still no answer.

On to her game, I pulled out my cell phone and turned on the flashlight application. Lighting my way down the darkened corridor, I cursed our absentmindedness at forgetting to change the light bulbs in the upstairs rooms.

"Maggie? Where'd you go?" I called again in a sing-song voice, a smile on my lips. "I'm going to find you and when I do, you'll pay the price." I went into the front left bedroom, the one that we had decided would be ours, and shined the light about but saw no one. A cardboard box with 'linens' scrawled on the side of it sat near the bed. The bare mattress leaned against the black metal bed frame. After checking the closet I found that it was still empty except for a few items of our clothing.

I quickly retreated and walked across the hall to the second bedroom. It would eventually be a home office but was currently serving as storage. A large rolled-up rug leaned on the wall in the corner and a few cardboard boxes sat next to it in the darkened room. A quick check of the closet produced nothing. No Maggie.

I was purposefully saving the back left bedroom for last. The room creeped me out and I hated the feeling it evoked. Surely it was all in my head, and yet, I couldn't shrug off the feeling of unease I felt there. I quickly searched the third bedroom and bathroom but both were empty.

The game of Hide and Seek was quickly losing its thrill. The sound of thunder pounded overhead while lightning lit the rooms for a second and then plunged them back into darkness. I pressed on, however, not wanting to steal Maggie's fun.

"Oh, Maggie, you're running out of places to hide now," I called into the shadows as I stood in the doorway of the dreaded murder room. I tried to shake off the dark feeling as I shined the light around the murky blackness of the room. The wooden rocking horse, the rusted metal bed frame, the painted flowers on the wall—all appeared as they had the first day when we'd arrived there. And yet, something seemed different. I found myself standing in the middle of the dark room, pivoting while holding my cell phone up, its flashlight illuminating everything in its beam. Suddenly the flashlight flicked off leaving me in complete darkness. I felt for the button on my phone and pressed it, but nothing happened.

The phone battery was dead.

Impossible as it had been charging for most of the evening. Frustrated, I tried pressing the button again. Nothing. With a sigh, I shoved the useless item into my jeans pocket and stood there, disoriented in the darkness. I could hear nothing, except for my breathing and the storm outside. Suddenly, I got the feeling that I wasn't alone. That eerie, heavy feeling always caused me to avoid this room. I felt the tiny hairs on the back of my neck stand up, my pulse thundering in my ears.

I took a shuffling step forward, trying to leave the space and find the hallway once again. Another step forward and I found myself stumbling into the rusted bed frame. I cursed under my breath as my shin throbbed. Surely that would leave a bruise. My mood, now completely soured, changed into one of complete horror as a flash of lightning right outside the window illuminated the dark room. For there in front of me stood a young woman, a teenager really, staring at me. She was wearing a long white nightgown and her dark hair hung down in front of her face, partially obscuring it from view. I saw her for only a second, during that quick flash of lightning, and then she was gone. Fear raced through me as I bolted from the room, bruised shins be damned.

"Matthew! What in God's name is going on up there?" I heard Maggie calling up the stairs. Disoriented and confused, I stumbled down the stairs two at a time and all but collapsed at the bottom, sucking in great gulps of air.

"Matthew! What happened?" Maggie asked as she bent over my sweaty and gasping form. "I've been waiting for you in the sitting room. Didn't you hear me call for you?"

"We have to leave." I gasped in between gulps of air. I sat up slowly, avoiding looking up the staircase to the second floor.

"Leave? But it's storming out. And besides, this is our home," Maggie tutted, helping me to my feet. "What happened? I told you I'd help with the bed linens."

When I said nothing, giving her a look instead, she said gently, "Why don't you just sit here and rest? You're a mess." She gently pressed me backward into my chair and I didn't resist, my thoughts still on the apparition I saw upstairs.

Maggie left the room, returning a moment later with a glass of water.

"Here," she smiled softly while handing me the glass, her eyes never leaving mine. I accepted it and drank the contents in three big gulps. The concern on my wife's face was evident, but what could I say? *Honey, I saw a ghost in the back bedroom.* Even to me, that sounded ridiculous. I sighed, my pulse slowly returning to normal.

"Here, watch something on my phone," she handed it to me. "I'll be back in a few minutes." I numbly took the phone she offered, but didn't use it. I just set it on the side table next to me and then leaned back, closing my eyes.

The next thing I knew, it was morning. The sun streamed through the open windows of the sitting room. I sat up quickly, looking around for Maggie. I must have fallen asleep in the chair last night, but where was Maggie?

In a rush, I shot out of the chair and went to find my wife. I called for her, annoyed at the irrational panic in my voice. Luckily, I found her sitting on the back porch, a steamy mug of coffee nestled in her hands. She looked up with a smile when she heard me open the screened door.

"Hey handsome," she greeted as the screen door slapped closed behind me.

"Where'd you go last night?" I asked as I sat down next to her.

"I went upstairs to put the sheets on the bed but when I came down to get you, you were already asleep. I knew you'd had a rough evening so I just let you sleep," Maggie explained, taking a sip of her usual vanilla-flavored coffee. She swallowed and then looked over at me. "So, what happened to you last night? You came down the stairs, pale as a ghost. I'd been calling for you but you must have not heard me."

I didn't want to tell her about the creepy woman I had seen in the murder room. It was just my overactive imagination. A ghost? Really? I felt like laughing just thinking about how absurd it all sounded. It had simply been a distortion of sudden light to my enlarged dark-adjusted pupils... right? Instead of saying all the crazy thoughts in my head aloud, I looked at her and shrugged.

"I ran into that rusty bed frame up in the back bedroom. I'll probably get tetanus now," I laughed, trying to deflect her questions. I pulled my pant leg up to study my wound. A dark bruise had already appeared on my shin. Maggie made a face and looked away, never one for blood and guts. I chuckled at her reaction and went inside to get some coffee, hoping that she wouldn't ask any more questions.

***

We worked throughout the day peeling wallpaper and scraping paint in the dining room. It was boring work and I quickly found my mind drifting to the diary that was still sitting on the table. I absently flicked through it, reading brief entries here and there.

There was nothing of note, just the adolescent musings of a young girl. Apparently, she liked a boy named Jonah. There were a lot of entries about him, daydreams by the sound of them. It was toward the back of the book that something caught my eye.

An entry, dated June 15th, 1892, roughly two weeks before the initial Tate axe murders. I sat down on a dining chair and read the old penciled scrawl.

"Today Papa started acting so strangely. I'm not sure what happened but it was as though his mind was somewhere else. I asked him a question about milking Bessie and he turned to me but his eyes seemed to look right through me. He acted like he couldn't hear me. I asked my question again and his face changed into an angry one. He growled at me and then smacked me across the face! Papa has never hurt me before! I ran away, crying, and avoided him the rest of the day."

The diary entry stopped, a sloppy *"S.T."* scrawled at the bottom. I quickly turned the page to find the next entry, this one dated three days before the murders.

It read: *"I am so scared. Papa isn't himself still and even Mama seems nervous when he is around. Mama tells us kids to go outside or go upstairs when he's around. He still has that look in his eyes. Like he's looking through you but his eyes are dead. I caught him pushing Mama up against the counter in the kitchen and whispering something in her ear. Mama had tears running down her face and she looked scared. I couldn't tell what Papa was saying, but Mama nodded at me to leave the room. I didn't want to leave her but if Papa saw me, he might hurt us both."*

What on Earth had happened to Thaddeus Tate during this time? I wondered. This was part of the story that I had never heard. This first-hand account was both informative and nerve-racking. What had caused Thaddeus to go mad and slaughter his own family? As far as I knew, he had been arrested the day after the murders but never spoke another word until his death, dangling from a noose in his prison cell.

I knew I should get back to peeling wallpaper but the diary seemed to call to me. I'd read a lot already and knew I was getting close to the day of the murder. Lacking the willpower to get back to work, I nervously turned the page and saw there was only one entry left.

The page was stained and smudged, but it read as follows: "*Tonight Mama sent us all to bed early because Papa was acting angry. He even threw a glass at the wall and shattered it! Mama looked worried. She told me to pack some clothes for a trip but asked me to be quiet about it. I can tell she is scared. I packed a few items for myself and my siblings and hid the suitcase under our bed. Mama came up to the bedroom a little while later and whispered in my ear. She told me that we were leaving that night after Papa fell asleep. I was to lie down with my brothers and sisters and rest until she came for us. I was asked not to tell anyone so I didn't scare the younger children. I told Mama I'd do my best and helped the younger ones get into their bedclothes. Now, as I write this, the children are sleeping and I am getting tired. I think I will rest like Mama said. Hopefully, Papa will fall asleep soon.*"

With a sigh, I closed the old journal grimly. I knew what had happened that night. Mrs. Tate and the children never made it out. They were hacked to death with an axe by their very own father.

I decided not to bring up the contents of the diary to Maggie. I put it back in the hole in the wall where she'd found it and then replaced the baseboard, deciding to leave the past in the past.

***

Later that night I lay in bed unable to sleep. My mind kept thinking about the diary. What did it all mean? What had made Thaddeus go crazy? Was it a head injury? A toxin of some kind in the house? Frustrated, I rolled over with a huff and listened to Maggie snore softly next to me.

I must have fallen asleep because the next thing I knew, I woke up with a start. The room was still shrouded in shadows and the alarm clock next to the bed glowed with green numbers. It was 3:23 in the morning. Still not sure what had awoken me, I sat up slowly so I didn't disturb

Maggie. It was only when I glanced at her side of the bed, I realized she wasn't even there. Had she awoken me when she got out of bed? Surely not or I would have seen her.

I climbed out of bed and went to find her. I called for her but got no response. She wasn't in the bedrooms or the bathroom so I headed downstairs. A quick search of the kitchen and dining room also turned up nothing. The sitting room was empty.

Confused, I pivoted looking all around me when suddenly I noticed that the back door was open, the screened door slightly ajar. I quickly made my way over to the door and stepped out onto the porch. Looking around, I saw nothing at first, and then, small and dim, a light flickered in the old barn. Why would Maggie be in the old barn in the middle of the night?

I quickly made my way toward the barn, tripping on stones and uneven terrain. The barn door swung open slightly on its rusty hinges as I stepped into the darkened interior. Testing the aged floorboards under my weight, I stepped lightly when they let out a slight groan. Irritated at myself for not bringing a flashlight with me, I cautiously took a step further into the dilapidated structure but then decided it was a stupid endeavor. It was pitch black in there and I couldn't see anything. I'd probably lose an eye if I kept going.

"Maggie?" I called into the inky blackness. Waiting for my eyes to adjust, I moved my head from side to side, straining to hear. I heard nothing except mice rustling in the old straw strewn about the barn floor and my ragged breath escaping my lungs. Where had Maggie gone?

Deciding to leave the barn, I turned around and headed back outside. I looked across the darkened yard again, casting a glance up at the house. It was then that I saw the ghostly apparition of the young girl staring out at me from that dreadful bedroom. I rubbed my eyes and looked again but she was gone.

Shaking my head, trying to clear my thoughts, I looked back over my shoulder toward the interior of the old barn. Nothing but blackness met my eyes. I must be going crazy. This was dumb. No ghost girl was watching me. Shaking off the feeling of unease, I rolled my eyes at my ridiculousness and headed back towards the house to find my wife.

Suddenly a movement to my right caught my attention in the moonlight. I jumped and was instantly on guard. I then noticed eyes watching me from the tall weeds surrounding the fallow field near the barn. The hair on the back of my neck stood at attention and I felt sweat forming on my forehead. What or who was watching me? The eyes continued to watch, gold and unblinking. I had no weapon on my person, nothing to defend myself if I should be attacked.

I slowly backed away from the eyes, stumbling and tripping slightly as I made my way through the darkness. Cursing myself again for not bringing the large red metal flashlight lying on the kitchen counter, I suddenly felt a hardness behind me. The barn!

The weather-roughened planks dug into my shoulders as I stood there staring back at the eyes. The barn door was somewhere to my left but I was afraid to look and take my eyes off of the creature staring back at me. Slowly sliding toward the direction of the door, I kept my eyes trained ahead of me, staring down the glistening, glowing pupils in the weeds. I stumbled suddenly, my foot caught on something heavy and hard. Bending slowly to release my foot from its prison, I felt cold metal ensnared in the overgrown grass around my legs. Never taking my eyes off of the creature across the yard, I felt around blindly at the object at my feet. My hands slid from cold metal to a long smooth handle. An old shovel? No! It was an axe! I grabbed the worn handle and stood back up just as the eyes seemed to be creeping closer to me, then closer still. My pulse quickened and I held the axe up like a baseball bat, ready to strike.

Chaos broke at that moment. Utter chaos! A shrill scream filled the darkness, assaulting my ears. The sound came from the house and I tore my gaze away from the wretched eyes of the creature that was creeping up on me ever so slowly. A glance at the house, toward the scream–Maggie! In a panic, I took off at a sprint in the direction of the old farmhouse. Behind me, I could hear the tall grass wrestling, but I dared not look at the beast behind me, surely gaining on me with each bound.

With a slam of the wood door behind me, I found myself in the darkened kitchen once again. I quickly turned to lock the door and noticed the eyes were gone. Had it been an animal?

A thump sounded on the worn planked floorboards above me. I looked up over my head, trying to narrow down the source of the sound. Our bedroom? No...the murder room. I gulped in fear, then slowly made my way towards the bottom of the stairs, axe still in hand. Where was Maggie? Why had she screamed? Was there someone or something else in the house? Questions swirled around in my head as I slowly climbed the stairs, their worn treads creaking softly underfoot.

I was halfway up the old staircase when I heard a loud moan, followed by a scraping sound and another thud. I wanted to call out for my wife but was afraid that the ghostly girl—the ghost that I prided myself in not believing in—would hear me. I felt a hysterical laugh welling up in my chest. When had I become so fixated on something that didn't even exist? Even though part of my brain told me that I was being absurd, the other part told me I was a mess of fear and trepidation. I shook my head, trying to clear my brain but the thoughts, the fear, kept swirling.

Finally climbing the last step, I quickly glanced around the door frame to our bedroom, but Maggie was still not in bed. Dragging the old axe at my side, I decided to check the hideous bedroom at the back of the house. The one room in the house I loathed the most.

As I approached the doorway, I pulled the tool up to my shoulder, ready to take on any intruder. Holding the axe like a Louisville Slugger, I slowly walked around the corner of the door and stepped into the moonlit interior of the murder room.

The scene in front of me stopped me in my tracks.

The young girl was standing there, leaning over Maggie's prostrate form. Maggie's eyes were closed and she wasn't moving except for the rise and fall of her chest with each breath. Blood poured from a gash on her forehead, making a dark puddle on the floor. The ghostly transparent girl turned to me at that moment, looking at me. It was then that I noticed half her face was missing, nothing left but a bloody, pulpy mess.

"Get away from my wife!" I demanded, rushing forward. I raised the axe in a threatening manner and yet the girl continued to look at me. Then suddenly a half grin appeared on her face and she turned, leaning over Maggie once again. Her arms extended out and she wrapped her hands around Maggie's neck. I watched in horror as she began squeezing, choking Maggie.

"No!" I screamed as I lunged. The apparition began silently laughing as I swung the axe, the blade slicing through the air. Again and again, I swung, and still the girl laughed. In a rage, I dropped the axe and pounced at the ghastly figure of the undead apparition and tried punching her. My fist went straight through her and the last thing I saw were her eyes staring at me, her broken and distorted face just inches from mine.

***

I don't remember how long I lay there on the floor of that horrible room but when I came to, sunlight poured through the windows. I was lying on the floor, staring up at the ceiling, when I heard someone coming. The next thing I saw were the feet of men entering the room. Some of the men started gagging, and some spoke into radios clipped to their shoulders. In a disoriented haze, I tried to sit up, to figure out what was going on. The police? Why were they here? Who had called them and why?

"Mr. Tate? Matthew Tate?" a uniformed officer asked, crouching next to me. I felt myself nod, my head woozy and disoriented.

"Mr. Tate, do you know what happened here? Are you hurt?" the young officer asked, assessing me. I just stared at him, confused.

"Mr. Tate, the handyman got here this morning to check some things you asked him to fix. Do you remember that?" the officer said. He nodded to someone behind me, then looked back at me.

"I don't remember," I replied, my mouth dry, my eyes burning. I raised my hands to wipe my eyes when I noticed the blood. My hands were covered in blood, sticky and red. In a panic, I looked back at the cop. "Where is Maggie? Where is my wife?"

"Sir, your wife is dead. You don't remember that?" the officer inquired. "You axed her to death last night. You're covered in her blood and still had the axe in your hands when we got here."

A moan, low and feral, escaped my lips. Dear God, what had I done...

5

THE PIT

I remember the day we signed on our new house like it was yesterday. My husband, Nick, and I sat around a large table, pens in hand. Our realtor stood in the corner of the small room absently playing on his cell phone while Nick and I talked excitedly to each other in nervous whispers. We sat there fidgeting, waiting for things to begin. The day had finally come.

Nick and I had been married for nearly five years and had always rented a house, unsure where we wanted to settle down. When I became pregnant with our daughter, Hannah, we decided to buy our first house and "put down roots" as the saying goes. We looked at a few houses in our small town in Ohio but decided we would like the country life better and decided to look at more rural properties.

The search became tiresome though as we toured house after house and just didn't find "The One". The houses either had way too many quirks, awkward layouts, or just didn't feel like home. This went on for over a year.

Finally, one early December day our realtor called us to tell us about a property that had just been listed. Three bedrooms, two and a half baths, 22 acres of forest and meadows, only forty minutes from the city where we both worked. It sounded perfect! We told the realtor we'd meet him there to check it out.

I remember the first time I saw the house as we drove up the long and winding driveway. It was perfect! A cozy cottage nestled in a pine forest, cedar siding freshly painted. Large windows overlooked the leafless early winter woods behind the house and down the half-mile-long driveway. We were instantly in love with it and hadn't even seen the inside yet!

The yard and surrounding land were covered in fallen leaves from the autumn, crunching under our feet as we made our way up the front walk toward the house. It was chilly that day, gray and overcast, typical of an Ohio December.

"Welcome!" our realtor beamed, "C'mon in. Take off your shoes. The seller just washed all the carpets," he said. My husband and I quickly obliged as we started looking around. Hannah, now two years old and always eager to explore, toddled off to inspect everything.

Needless to say, the house was perfect for us! Yes, it needed some updating inside to make it our own but the layout and coziness felt like home. We put in an offer then and there, fingers crossed that this was the one. Finally, two days later, our realtor called to announce that the seller had accepted our offer and the house was ours as long as loans and inspections all went well. We were ecstatic, instantly calling friends and family to update them, going to Home Depot for paint swatches, and getting empty boxes and rolls of packing tape.

After nearly two months of paperwork, finalizing the mortgage loan, and packing all our belongings we were ready for Closing Day! We just wanted them to give us the keys so we could begin our dream life!

The excitement was almost palpable as we sat in the small room with the large table, waiting for the seller to sign the paperwork. Nick and I were nervous about spending so much money yet nearly giddy about owning our first house. When the seller arrived with his realtor, the paperwork began. I have never signed my name so many times in such a short period and by the end, my hand was exhausted, but the house was finally ours!

As we stood to shake hands and say our goodbyes, the seller, an older man with a paunch that sagged over his waistband, paused in the doorway.

"Oh, I almost forgot! There is a small graveyard on the property, deep in the woods," he said, "but don't worry about it. It's all legal with the county. Just thought I'd mention it so that you didn't trip over it. It's pretty old and the markers are almost level with the ground. You could walk right over them and not even know." And with that, he and his realtor were gone, disappearing down the hallway.

"Oh great! We've just inherited some dead people." Nick said, rolling his eyes. "Shouldn't they have told us that earlier?"

"Yes," our realtor said, looking somewhat annoyed at what had just happened. "We should have seen it when pulling county records and researching the property. I saw no mention of it."

"Maybe he's just trying to scare us?" I said with a shrug. "It's just a couple of skeletons. How much trouble can they be? Just charge them rent if it makes you feel better." I grinned.

Nick looked at me, rolled his eyes again, and said, "I guess it's too late now. It's ours. And you're right. They are just a few bones not bothering anyone."

The next few weeks flew by. Each day was exhausting, moving boxes, and driving back and forth from the old house to the new one. By now it was early February and we wondered "Who would move in the middle of Winter?" Oh wait, we did! We would just shrug, put on our snow boots, and plod back and forth from truck to house carrying all our earthly possessions. We were so busy that the graveyard was soon forgotten.

Slowly, winter turned to spring, and the forest came to life again. Most of the house was set up and organized but the yard was another story. The house had sat empty for a few years and the unkempt yard had been reclaimed by the surrounding forest. A thick layer of leaves covered the ground had snuffed out any grass that may have once been there. When the days became warm and dry enough, we set to work, raking, clipping, pruning. Hannah would toddle around in the yard while we worked, investigating insects or wildflowers. Before long, the yard was starting to take shape again.

I remember it was a Sunday, the weekend after Mother's Day, when I was out raking some leaves some distance from the house. We wanted to put in a chicken coop and that particular spot was nice and flat, open enough to put a coop and chicken run but still shaded by the tall oaks and maples. I had set out that morning to rake all the leaves away and begin marking out exactly where I wanted my coop to go.

The sun was out, warming my back, as I raked the thick layer of detritus out of my way. I was deep in thought about the upcoming workday when suddenly my rake scraped over something hard under the packed leaves. Curious, I knelt to see what it was. Brushing some loose soil away, I eventually found the edge of an old board. I used my fingers to dig around the edge of it so I could pull it out and discard it. That is when I discovered there were more boards and they were nailed together. Curiosity piqued, I went to the garden shed to retrieve a small shovel and went back to the buried wooden planks.

"Whatcha digging over there?" Nick asked, Hannah in his arms, as he walked over to me.

"I don't know. I found a couple of boards all nailed together. They were under all the leaves and a few inches of dirt." I said, wiping sweat off my brow with the back of my hand.

"Oh! What if it's the graveyard?" Nick said, tickling Hannah in the belly. She let out a giggle.

"Buried like four inches underground?" I laughed. "Doubtful. Besides, that guy said the graveyard was deep in the woods somewhere." I jabbed the shovel in the dirt and scooped some more dirt away from the planks. "It's probably just some junk laying out in the yard that got covered up over time."

"Well, if you find anything exciting, come find us," Nick said, turning to walk back towards the house. "We are going to go get some applesauce. Aren't we, Hannah?"

"Applesauce!" she crooned. With a grin, the two were off and I got back to work.

Humming to myself, I kept scraping off damp earth from the planks on the ground. I finally realized it was an old door, tossed on the ground, and buried over time. The door was small, roughly three feet wide and four feet long. Figuring I'd just throw it in the junk pile we had started accumulating with remodeling fallout, I continued to dig around the edges. Sliding the edge of the shovel's blade under the edge of the crude door, I used it as a lever in an attempt to pry the door off of the ground. After a few attempts, the door still wouldn't move. I continued scraping off the dirt from its surface, the door almost completely exposed now. As I went to scoop yet another load of damp earth off, the shovel's blade made a metallic clunk when it hit something buried, just out of view.

"What now?" I muttered, bending to unearth the source of the metallic sound. It was then that I realized it was a padlock. A padlock attached to the old door, locking it shut. Confused, I sat back on my heels, surveying the scene before me.

Was it an old cellar? But why padlock a cellar? Maybe it was a cap on an old well! Yes, I told myself, *it was just an old well, locked to keep children from falling in.* I nodded to myself, assured that the door was exactly that.

Deciding to get a drink and tell Nick about the well, I headed back to the house.

"Find anything interesting?" Nick asked, wiping applesauce off of Hannah's satisfied face.

"I think it's the well cover. There is a padlock and everything to keep people from falling in." I said, pouring myself a tall glass of lemonade from the fridge.

"The well?" Nick said, making a face. "The well is on the other side of the house, babe. Remember?"

"Oh yeah!" I said, suddenly remembering the inspector saying something about it. "Well, then what do you think it is? Like, who would lock a cellar? Somebody *really* wanted to keep their canned goods safe." I added sarcastically.

"People lock their cellars all the time, so weirdos don't go into their homes."

"Well, yeah, but that's cellar doors that are attached to the houses' basements," I said, in between mouthfuls of lemonade. "This one isn't anywhere close to the house."

"Fine. Then let's go look," Nick complied.

A few moments and a crowbar later, Nick and I stood next to the mysterious door on the ground. Hannah, oblivious to all of it, meandered nearby playing with wildflowers. I stood by and watched as Nick used the crowbar to pop the lock off, his forearms straining under the effort. After a few attempts, we heard the old wood groan and then crack. The board holding the lock split in two rendering the lock useless. The lock was stainless steel but the hinges and latch looked much older. The rust covering them blended in with the damp dirt and leaves that had kept them hidden for so long.

"Ready?" Nick said, wiggling his eyebrows at me and grinning. "You know this is just going to be some stupid shallow hole somebody dug to use as a playhouse or something. Don't get too excited."

"Whatever. Don't be a Debbie Downer." I joked, playfully shoving him out of the way so I could open the door. "I read too many Nancy Drew mysteries as a kid. Until proven otherwise, this door is mysterious and holds lots of secrets."

Nick laughed then, used to my morbid curiosity. He bowed and swept his hand in a gallant gesture. "Please, ladies first."

With a soft grunt, I pulled at the door. It was heavy from ground water and dirt but I felt it groan on its hinges as it slowly opened. I let go of it and it fell open on the ground. I heard Nick gasp next to me and we both stood there looking at what was under the door.

There before us, dug out of the ground, was a stairway, rocky and uneven, disappearing down into the darkness.

"See? A cellar!" Nick announced. "Told you." I rolled my eyes at him and then turned, stepping down the first two steps. I couldn't see where they ended due to the darkness.

"You have a headlight?" I asked him. He nodded and ran over to the garage to get it. When he got back he handed it to me along with a flashlight.

"Thanks. Watch Hannah," I smiled up at him, sticking the headlight around my head. "I'll be back."

"We'll be waiting," he nodded, eyeing Hannah playing with dandelions.

I started my descent, figuring it would be five or six stairs down but in reality, it was nearly fourteen. I counted them under my breath as I slowly made my way down the uneven surface. The stairs themselves were made of a mix of stones and cinder blocks. The walls of the tunnel were dirt lending to the damp, earthy smell that surrounded me. Daylight was gone, soon replaced by a murky darkness and I flipped on the headlamp and the flashlight, illuminating my way. I shined my light around the narrow passageway and realized it wasn't a cellar. At least not in the typical sense.

The stairway had finally ended and led to a narrow tunnel roughly twenty feet long. The ceiling of the tunnel was only about five feet high so I was forced to duck my head as I made my way forward. Spiderwebs floated in the breeze I caused as I walked by and I tried not to think about their eight-legged inhabitants. At the end of the tunnel, the floor muddy in areas from groundwater was a second door with another padlock.

"What the.....?" I whispered to myself. Confused and somewhat delightfully creeped out, I reached up and tried the lock. It held fast. I shook the door but it merely rattled on its hinges. This door was also made of planks, but older ones that had already started to rot away on the ends, leaving small gaps at the bottom and top of the door. I shined my light through the upper cracks and saw more darkness. I could feel cool air moving through the gap and knew there was an open chamber beyond it.

Deciding to turn back to tell Nick what I'd found, I quickly retraced my steps, tripping a few times in my haste.

"Well.....?" He asked expectantly when I resurfaced from the hole. Hannah watched me from her perch on his hip.

"You need to call your sister or mom to come and watch Hannah," I exclaimed, out of breath from excitement and exertion. "There is another padlocked door and a room beyond it!"

"Seriously?" he asked, curiously looking down the descending stairway, totally interested now. "I'm going to go look." He shoved Hannah into my arms and I handed him the headlight and flashlight. As he descended into the pit, I called his sister, Sarah, who lived a few minutes away. She was instantly excited about the mysterious hole and said she'd be right there.

Nick re-emerged from the stairwell a few moments later, muddied but excited. "Okay, so it's not a cellar but I have no idea what it is! We need the crowbar again!"

"Maybe it's a fallout shelter or bunker of some kind?" I suggested as Sarah pulled up the driveway, tires spitting gravel as she skidded to a halt. Jumping out of her Jeep, she ran over to us.

"So you found a secret tunnel in your yard?" she asked, already looking down the hole. The excitement on her face was evident. "Can I go look?" Nick and I nodded, and with an impish grin, she took the lights and made her decent, me hot on her trail.

"So you were just cleaning up the yard and found this...this spooky tunnel?" she asked, shining her light around the small space.

"Yes, I thought it was just a well cap or a cellar of some kind," I said, shining the light on the door at the end of the passageway. "I don't know what it is but I don't think it's a cellar. Maybe like a bunker? You know, like for an end-of-days scenario?"

"Maybe," Sarah agreed, giving the door a good shake.

"Here, allow me," I said, holding up the crowbar. Sarah stepped out of the way and I slid the iron bar under the lock and pried. After a few attempts, the screws holding the lock plate in place slowly gave way and it fell off, the door falling open a few inches. I looked at Sarah and she excitedly nodded, so I pushed the door open the rest of the way and shined the light inside.

Through the now open doorway, we could see a room, roughly twenty feet wide by thirty feet long. The ceiling was approximately six feet or so high. The floor seemed to be dirt and was covered by a rug of green plastic grass, like Astro Turf. It was dirty and covered the lumpy uneven floor. Along the walls were crude wooden shelves, some filled with old Mason jars of moldering vegetables and stewed meats. From the look of them, they had been placed there some time ago. Each was covered with a thick layer of dust and cobwebs and the water level in each jar had seemed to evaporate to nearly nothing. An army green rucksack sat on one shelf full of something cloth and an old suitcase was on the top shelf. A few books lay strewn haphazardly on a shelf collecting dust.

I looked around the space, taking in each detail, wondering why someone would collect such random items and keep them locked underground. The room took on a creepy feel as the only light came from the flashlight and headlamp, both casting shadows about the small space.

"Look at that old lantern," Sarah said, pointing to an antique metal lantern with a crack in the glass. An old shovel leaned against the wall in the far corner. "This is super weird. The whole thing." She paused to sniff the air. "It also smells funky."

I sniffed the air then and noticed an earthy dirt smell mixed with something mildly unpleasant, like mildew or rotten vegetation.

"Right? Why lock this place up in the first place, much less, put two locks on two different doors?" I commented, noticing some boards leaning up against the far wall.

"To keep somebody out?"

"Or to keep something in," I shrugged, my imagination going wild. Sarah just rolled her eyes and grinned.

"Stop it. There isn't anything exciting here. Just a room full of old crap." Sarah dusted off her hands even though she hadn't touched anything. "C'mon. Let's go tell Nick what we found."

A short time later, sitting around the table in the kitchen eating some hotdogs and potato chips, we told Nick all about what we'd found. He'd brought Hannah in for her nap and said he'd explore it later. In the meantime, I'd closed the door back over the hole to keep people and animals out. We came up with different scenarios about why the stuff was down there and why it was locked up but none of them made any real sense. We finally gave up and after Sarah left, I cleaned up the kitchen, the pit forgotten for the moment.

Later that night, as Nick snored softly next to me, I found myself awake, my mind racing. Sleep eluded me and after a while of tossing and turning, I finally gave up and got out of bed. I went into the living room and looked out the picture window at the night shadows around me. Without much forethought, I walked out onto the deck and sat in one of the gliders, looking up at the moon. Night sounds surrounded me–crickets chirping, frogs singing, leaves rustling. A gentle breeze blew past me, a slight chill traveling down my neck. I was wide awake and knew I wouldn't be falling asleep any time soon. My eyes watched the woodline for animals and then slowly made their way toward the pit across the yard. Drawn to the mysterious hole, I decided to walk out there and look again. Mind made up, I went back inside to grab a hoodie, flashlight, and rubber boots and headed towards the door in the ground.

"This is dumb," I muttered to myself as I opened the door and shined the light down the narrow stairway. "I just want to sleep and all I can think about is this hole in the ground." The passageway appeared as it had earlier that day, just darker at the opening. I questioned my judgment of doing this alone in the middle of the night but it was just a room underground, wasn't it?

I made it to the second door and pushed it open, the musty rotting smell assaulting my nostrils again. Dust motes danced in front of my flashlight beam and the room was silent except for the sound of my breathing.

Something crunched under my foot and I quickly looked down to see the remains of some beetle that must have been scurrying across my path. Scraping the goo off of the bottom of my boot, I stepped into the room as I had earlier with my sister. Looking around with the flashlight beam, I noticed that nothing had changed, not that I had expected it to. The canned goods still sat on the shelf, the old suitcase lay on the top shelf, and books in a pile.

My eyes were drawn back to the suitcase. I wondered what was inside, unsure why Sarah and I hadn't looked earlier. I walked across the uneven dirt floor over to the old wooden shelf and reached up for the suitcase. A cloud of dust flew into my face and I coughed and sneezed for a few moments, standing there holding the old suitcase. Finally catching my breath, I squatted down and laid the suitcase on the dirt floor. Flashlight in hand, I tried to pry the rusty old locks open. The suitcase was a soft-sided one, not the hard plastic kind popular with travelers these days. The fabric looked to have once been a dark blue color with some kind of small geometric design but it was too dusty and moldy for me to determine in the darkened room. The first lock sprung open easily enough but the second one gave me some difficulty. With a sigh, I was forced to lay down the flashlight so that I could use both hands on the lock. With some effort, the rusty lock gave way and I was able to open it. Picking up the flashlight again, I shined the beam on the suitcase and slowly raised the lid an inch.

"What are you doing out here, babe?" Nick said from the doorway, causing me to jump and drop the lid closed. I hadn't even heard him come down the tunnel. He stood there, baby monitor in hand, looking bleary-eyed, hair messy.

"I'm sorry," I said, my pulse slowly returning to normal. "I couldn't sleep and decided to come check this place out again."

"It's like one in the morning. Maybe you should just come back to bed. I saw that the front door was open and came outside looking for you," Nick said, stifling a yawn.

With a sigh, I knew he was right. I had work tomorrow and I'd be a zombie if I didn't get some sleep. I latched the suitcase again but decided to take it with me so that I could check it out after work in better lighting.

***

The next day, I couldn't get my mind off the creepy stairway and room buried in the wooded area of my yard. It was the topic of conversation around the lunch table and throughout the day, coworkers would stop by my desk and ask questions about it or tell me their theories about the room's origins. I heard everything from an alien fallout bunker to a room where they locked up some crazy man who was unfit to live among the general public. I had some good laughs but as the clock slowly ticked and the hours passed, I was ready to get home and investigate further. This was more intriguing than searching for the old graveyard the man had told me about.

Later that evening, after the kitchen was cleaned up from dinner, I decided to open the suitcase. A little too excited about it, I spread an old bed sheet over the kitchen table and laid the suitcase on it. It was so dusty and dingey I didn't want to just lay it on the table. Nick was playing with Hannah in the living room but kept coming in to ask if I was ready to open it. When I announced I was, he came into the kitchen, and together we raised the lid.

Inside were some papers and photos, an old book, some random pieces of jewelry, and an old red silk scarf.

"What is this stuff?" I said, picking up a photograph. The picture appeared old, taken back in the 1970s or early 80s. In the photo, a young woman was leaning against a white car, the big boxy kind that was so famous back then. She had long dark hair, hanging loose, and a huge smile on her face. Her shorts and sleeveless shirt showed that it was summer when the photo was taken.

Another photograph showed the same woman, but this time, she looked more serious and her face took up most of the frame. Her hair was pulled back in a ponytail and she wore a thin gold chain around her neck, complete with a sapphire pendant that matched her eyes. I flipped the photo over and saw "Patty, 1978" written in pencil on the back. I checked the first picture and found "Pat, Aug 1976." *Who was this woman? I* wondered to myself.

I flipped through the other three photos but they didn't reveal anything. One was just a view of a forest at the edge of a gravel road, one was an old house with chipping yellow paint. On the back was written, "Home, 1976" but it did not indicate where the house was located. The last photo looked like a blurry hand, as though someone had put their hand over the lens to avoid their picture being taken. I could see trees in the background, possibly the same woods from the other photo.

I set the photos to the side in a stack and continued searching the suitcase for clues. There were a couple of pieces of paper. A receipt from a grocery store possibly. It had faded over time and was hard to read. The second piece of paper looked to be a parking pass from 1985 and the last was a flyer for a senior prom at the local high school... dated May 25, 1985. I was confused and wondering why these random items were in an old suitcase, locked in some mysterious underground chamber. I picked up the book next and something fell out. I glanced down and saw that two thin plastic cards had fallen out and lay scattered on the table. I picked one up and noticed it was a driver's license. A state of Ohio driver's license for Patricia Anne Headly. It expired in 1979. The small blurry photo appeared to be the girl in the photographs. Who was Patricia Headly and why were her things in this suitcase?

I picked up the other piece of plastic and flipped it over. It was a 1985 school ID for the local high school, the same one that had held the senior prom. The name on the ID read Chelsea Lynn Struthers. The picture on the ID, small and grainy, showed a smiling young woman with green eyes and blonde streaked hair pulled back in a red scarf. Large star-shaped earrings dangled from each ear lobe.

"Who were you?" I muttered to myself, wondering how the two women were connected if they were connected at all. I pulled out my cell phone and Googled Chelsea's name. A few random hits popped up but nothing that made any sense. I then tried "Chelsea Lynn Struthers, 1985" and the name of the high school. My heart skipped a beat when the results appeared on my screen. My hands shaking, I read the headlines from a local newspaper article dated back to the 80's. "Local Teen Missing After High School Prom".

I clicked on the link and read it in disbelief.

Per the article, Chelsea had been seen last at the prom, dancing and laughing with friends. Some students claimed to have seen her talking to a man in a green Ford pickup truck in the parking lot. That was the last verified sighting of her. Her family was distraught and anxious for any news on her whereabouts. A reward for information was offered but no new leads had come in and the case remained cold.

I looked for more articles but the ones I did find just had the same information. Nothing new since 1986. With a frown, I decided to look up Pat Headly's name. With dismay, I found news articles from 1998. "Twenty-year-old Cold Case Still Baffles Detectives", "Ohio Teacher Missing over Two Decades" and "Where is Patty Headly?"

My hands began shaking, my heart was pounding, and I felt my anxiety rise. Why were there items belonging to two missing women in a suitcase locked in a room underground? And then it hit me like a freight train.

Because it wasn't a cellar for random items. It was a tomb.

When the truth hit me, I let out a shaking scream and Nick came running. Without saying a word, I dropped my phone and the women's items and ran from the house, across the yard, and down into the pit. Nick came after me, Hannah in his arms, flashlight in his hand.

"What is going on?" he asked, handing me the flashlight. I could hardly breathe, my breath coming out in panting puffs. I was shaking and felt as though I was going to vomit.

"Call the police," I said finally, breathing deeply.

"The police?" Nick said confused, already pulling his cell phone out.

"Yes!" I nearly shouted, turning around to head deeper into the tunnel. "Just do it! I'll explain later." With that, I disappeared into the room at the end of the passageway.

I stood there, looking around for a moment, breathing hard, desperate to find the secrets hidden there. Nothing was exciting about the shelving and the rug was just an old sheet of fake grass, but what about the boards leaning up against the far wall? I walked toward the boards, finally stepping on the fake grass for the first time. The ground underneath it was lumpy and uneven and the fake strands of grass made funny crunchy noises when I walked over them. I never liked Astro Turf and disliked it even more in this dark, dank room. I made a face of disgust and continued toward the boards leaning up against the wall. I was unsure what was behind them and was apprehensive.

Kneeling in front of the boards, I mentally braced myself for what I was about to do. I took a deep breath and with one swift motion, I pulled the boards down.

Nothing.

There was nothing behind them, just cobwebs and some dead insects. I breathed a sigh of relief and yet..... Why was that suitcase in here, locked and hidden away? I must be missing something. I looked up at the ceiling and saw nothing out of the ordinary. The walls looked undisturbed and sturdy. I walked towards the middle of the room, across that disgusting fake grass, when suddenly, my foot sunk into a soft spot under the rug. I fell forward and landed on my knees and palms on the lumpy green surface. It was then that I felt the hard ground under my right knee and hand, but that the ground under my left side seemed to sink some. Could it be that easy? Could the missing girls be hidden in plain sight?

I knew I should wait for the police to show up but I felt compelled to keep looking. I struggled to get up, my left foot and hand sinking into the unsupported green rug. I finally made it to the edge of the rug and stood up. With a deep breath, I grasped the corner of the rug, cringing at the feel of the fake grass, and began pulling it back from the dirt floor.

I let out a cry when I shined my light on the area at my feet. There, in front of me were two small pits, roughly two feet by six feet and just two feet deep. In each one, lay the mummified remains of two women, their bodies dried out and shriveled, hair still laying around their shoulders. Patty and Chelsea.

I felt vomit churning in my stomach and ran from the room. Falling into a pile of blubbering and shaking mess, I cried, and rocked myself, completely in shock. Dear God, how long had they been down there? Who had put them there?

I remember the police coming, their lights flashing and casting blue and red shadows over my house and yard. I remember yellow crime scene tape making a perimeter around the pit. I remember them taking the suitcase with the girls' photos and papers as evidence. I remember going down to the station to provide my official statement. Past that, everything was a blur. The news stories, the press converging at the end of our long driveway, the dark stain on our perfect new home.

It was a few days later when Nick and I got asked to come down to the police station to finalize some paper-work. We climbed the stairs of the plain tan building, ready to be done with this ordeal as quickly as possible. After approaching the front desk to check in, we were asked to wait in the lobby for the detective. We sat in the blue plastic chairs in the lobby and waited. After a few moments, the front door of the police station opened and two officers came in, guiding an older man wearing handcuffs. At first, I didn't recognize him. And then he looked over at me and smiled.

"I see you found my graveyard! I told you it was deep in the woods," he said, and with that, he let out a cackling laugh and disappeared into the back of the station with the officers.

6

THE BELLS OF ST. ANDREWS CEMETERY

Ohio, 1823

It had been a long day for John Sutton, the gravedigger, and groundskeeper of St. Andrews Cemetery at the edge of town. There had been three deaths that week alone which was highly unusual for the small farming community. Usually, John had to dig a grave every few weeks or so, depending on the time of year. During harvest season, he'd seen a fair share of accidental manglings from farm equipment. During the colder winter months influenza and other ailments always seemed to bring more work for him.

It was well after dark and he was nearly finished filling in the final grave. With the shortened days of late October, he had been working by lantern light for the last hour or so. The moon above was partially covered with clouds, casting shadows through the trees and headstones nearby. Other than the sound of the shovel scraping on the loose soil near the freshly filled grave, the night was silent. A gentle breeze, occasionally stirring the leaves into a frenzy of orange and red, added a mild chill in the air.

John stood up straight to stretch his back, having been stooped over for the past few hours filling the three graves. His stomach growled, reminding him that he hadn't eaten anything since before noon. He was almost done with this dark job, so he continued, filling his shovel and dumping dirt into the pit before him.

He'd dug all the graves yesterday, with the help of a young boy from town looking to make a little coin. Tonight, though, John was on his own. The funeral services had been scattered throughout the day, causing him to work late into the night to finish.

Jedidiah Green, aged 54 years, had succumbed to influenza as had his young grandson, Timothy. The third grave belonged to Miss Annie Flynn, aged 23, who had died in her sleep after a short bout of sickness. John had never met Annie personally but he had known Jedidiah.

John sighed now, as he stood filling in his friend's grave. He had spent time with old Jed numerous times before, playing cards, fishing, and even learning to whittle. John knew he'd miss his friend, and perhaps that was why he seemed to be taking his time now, filling the grave slowly and reflecting. John bent and grabbed the burial pole, meant to hold a bell on a thin rope to signal if someone had inadvertently been buried alive. He pushed it down into the freshly turned soil near the newly dug grave.

The town had only recently been using the burial bells after hearing reports of people being prematurely interred. A thin rope or twine was attached to the inside of a coffin or the corpse's wrist and then fed through a metal pipe inserted into the ground near the grave. The other end of the string was then attached to a small bell. The idea was that, if buried whilst still alive, the person in the coffin would pull the string, causing the bell to ring and initiate rescue efforts.

John couldn't imagine the horror of being buried alive: the claustrophobic feeling, knowing you had limited oxygen, the unrelenting darkness. No one would know you were alive, trying desperately to maneuver around in the blackened confines, your movements inhibited by the narrow space.

Patting down another clump of dirt on his friend's grave, John Sutton shivered. Perhaps it was the dark thoughts parading through his mind, or the quickly dropping temperature around him.

It was then that he heard a light rain begin to fall, and felt it pelting the wide brim of his hat. The flame in his lantern swayed slightly behind the safety of its glass, casting awkward shadows about.

John felt the dampness slowly seeping into his shirt, making its way to his skin. Quickening his pace, he dumped the last few shovelfuls of earth onto the fresh mound in front of him. He quickly attached the bell to the end of the frayed twine threaded through the metal burial pole. Satisfied with his work, he paused for a moment to say his final goodbyes to his friend.

The drizzle continued to fall as John picked up the shovel and lantern and began the trek back toward the gardener's shed at the back of the churchyard. He'd only made it a few paces when he heard it.

A tinkle of a bell, soft yet distinct.

He paused, thinking surely he'd imagined it. When he heard nothing more, he shook his head slightly and took another step. Another jingling sound assaulted his ears. John stopped in his tracks, frozen, listening. The hair on the back of his neck stood on end and his pulse quickened.

Dear God, what had he done? In a panic, John turned and quickly made his way back to Jed's grave. He stood there for a moment, his breath coming out in quick puffs, staring at the bell. It didn't budge.

John waited, watching the bell as if his life depended on it. Waiting, panicking. Worried that he had prematurely interned his dear friend, John felt as though he would vomit. After what felt like an hour, sitting in the drizzle, the ground damp with water, John heard nothing else save the drops of rain hitting the ground.

"I'm going mad," John muttered to himself. He slowly got to his feet, wiping at the seat of his pants to knock off what remnants of dirt he could. "I'm simply going mad."

He shook the water droplets from his hat and then placed it on his head once again. Bending to retrieve his discarded shovel and lantern a second time, John paused by the bell once more. Had he imagined it? Or was he just simply worn out and exhausted from all the emotional and physical turmoil of the past few days?

The sickness had first made an appearance a week or so prior in the neighboring town of Ghent. Influenza from the sounds of it. John had heard reports of nearly ten people who had already succumbed to the disease and more had fallen ill. It didn't take long for the epidemic to spread, making John's friends and family ill and sequestered in their beds. He'd already buried three people who'd fallen to the sickness. One last week and now Jed and his grandson. John's brother, Jamie, was currently feeling ill and John feared that he would catch it and endure the same fate as his friend. Who would bury John? Surely one of the younger men in the village would step forward and take over the groundwork and digging of graves at the old St. Andrews Cemetery.

No one knew for sure if Annie Flynn had the same sickness that was spreading through their town, but John assumed she had. He'd heard Mrs. McClane, the local dressmaker and town busybody, saying that Annie had been running a fever and having difficulty breathing. The diarrhea started a couple of days later. Within two days, Annie was dead.

Another gust of cool October air whizzed past John, bringing with it a misty rain that sent a shiver down his spine. Straightening his coat, John turned and began walking towards the garden shed, shovel and lantern in hand. His mind wandered back to thoughts about how it must feel to be buried alive.

He'd heard stories over the years of people who had been prematurely interred, buried and quickly forgotten by everyone except family. One story stood out in his mind the most, however, one that had kept him awake all night when he'd first heard it. As it had been told to him, a man from down south somewhere had died under suspicious circumstances and the family wanted to verify that their dear father had indeed been buried with an heirloom pocket watch as he'd wished. The pocket watch's whereabouts had come into question when it had turned up for sale at a general store three towns over. The police had exhumed the body after much argument and requests from the family and what they found was so hideous, so horrible, that John shivered even thinking about it. For on the inside of the coffin's lid were claw marks, deeply etched in the pine wood. The man's face was distorted in a look of sheer terror, mouth agape, as though in a silent scream. The newspaper reported that the man's hands were bloodied, his fingernails peeled back and broken from his efforts to escape his plight. As for the pocket watch, it was indeed missing from the coffin, apparently pilfered by a rapacious funeral guest.

Because of stories like the man with the pocket watch, John and other gravediggers like him, had started implementing the use of the funeral bells. It had only been nine months or so since John had tied his first bell on, and as of yet, he had never had one ring. He'd had a couple fall off, even had one stolen. But never had one rang. Just the thought of one ringing from the efforts of a subterranean tug made John's skin crawl.

Now, as he slowly sidestepped past a granite tombstone, chipped and moldering with age, the night was silent save for the misty rain that continued to fall. He'd barely taken four or five steps when he stopped dead in his tracks.

There, just past the sound of the rain hitting the fallen leaves covering the ground, came the sound of a bell. Small and tinny, the sound assaulted John's ears as though it were as loud as a steam engine's whistle. He turned abruptly to look behind him and saw nothing except tombstones and the three freshly turned graves.

He swiftly walked back to Jed's grave, his boots slipping occasionally in the dirt and mud underfoot. Again, he paused, staring at the bell, willing it to–what? He almost wanted it to ring, to prove that he wasn't going mad. And yet, if it *did* ring, it would mean that he had just finished burying his dear friend alive. John swallowed hard at the thought, his pulse quickening.

The seconds turned into minutes and still, John watched, waiting, but nothing happened. No sounds other than the rain and his own quickened breathing. He was about to give up and go home when suddenly behind him, he heard the bell chime again, soft and delicate. He sat up on his haunches and listened and there it was again. The bell. But it wasn't Jed's bell as he had originally thought.

It was coming from the direction of Annie Flynn's grave.

Quickly, John launched to his feet and stumbled towards Annie's graveside, slipping on the wet grass as he went. Out of breath from exertion and fear, John stopped in front of Annie's burial bell, bent over at the waist and breathing hard. Had he really heard it? His mind swam, his thoughts muddied.

He grabbed the bell and gave the attached string a slight tug, waiting for it to be reciprocated. Suddenly, to his horror, he felt it. The slightest tug from the other end of the rope.

"Dear God, forgive me!" he cried out as he desperately began removing the dirt from the freshly turned grave. "Someone help me!" he screamed into the night, hoping, willing anyone to hear his plea and come to his aid.

Feverishly he dug into the dirt, shovelful after shovelful. Time seemed to pass at a snail's pace and yet no one came to help. It was near midnight, and surely everyone was home, safe and dry in their beds. Everyone except John Sutton. Through sweat and tears, his mournful cries caught in his chest, he pressed on.

Digging deeper and deeper, he tried desperately to make his way to poor Annie Flynn before it was too late. Surely her blood would be on his hands. He continued to scream for help but his pleas were drowned out by the sound of the wind and rain. The rain began to fall in earnest now, filling divots in the dirt, and pooling around his shovel. John's back ached, his muscles protesting with each strain of the mud-laden shovel, but still, he pressed on. The ringing sounds came again causing John to pause for a moment and then push on with renewed fervor. He was exhausted, sweating, his hands and arms trembling with each thrust of the shovel.

Every second counted and if John was to save poor Annie, he must quicken his efforts. As he continued to dig, he watched in horror as the rain caused mud from the surface to fall in chunks, filling the grave as he was emptying it. With a growl of frustration, John continued, digging and scooping mud and water out of his way, as he searched for the coffin.

Finally, when he thought his body would give out, his shovel hit something hard. Hoping it was the coffin lid, John bent down, feeling under the muddied water swirling at his feet. To his dismay, he only found a rock. Angry and frustrated, he flung it from the grave and continued digging. His breathing was labored and his head throbbed, but still, he did not give up. When he thought he would never make it, his shovel hit something again, this time causing a hollow wooden sound. The coffin!

Almost yelling in triumph, John was far from opening the casket. The mud and dirt still covered most of the surface, making it impossible to open. He gave three taps of the shovel on the coffin, hoping to give Annie some reassurance that she was not alone, and then continued digging out the lid.

The rain continued to fall, filling the hole almost as fast as John was emptying it. His lantern, sitting on the grass at the surface of the grave, did little to light his work, but merely cast shadows into the pit. John thought about getting the lantern to light his way but thought against it. The sides of the grave were slowly eroding as the deluge above continued. He could feel the water filling his boots now, and every time he shifted the mud made sucking sounds, threatening to pull his boots off his feet.

After feverishly digging for a few more moments, John had the top half of the coffin lid unearthed. To his frustration, as he tried to smash open the wooden chamber, his shovel merely slid off the slick surface, leaving nothing more than scratches.

Desperation filled him, and he cried out. Surely the poor girl under his feet was struggling to breathe. How long had she been underground now? Three, maybe four hours? If only he had checked her again. If only he had... John paused for a moment, thinking.

How was this his fault? He wasn't the one that had determined the poor girl had died. It wasn't he who had placed her in the coffin, dressed in her best gown and laid out for her family to say goodbye. He had merely been called upon to transport her remains to the cemetery and inter her in the family plot. He never opened the coffins, never had a peek. He'd heard of others who would look. Other gravediggers would take a peek under a pretty woman's clothes, maybe steal a bracelet or earbobs. After all, was the decedent really in need of such frivolities? John would think not, but it wasn't his job to determine. Such activities went against his moral fortitude. But morals aside, it was his job now to save this young woman from her current predicament.

The rain continued its unrelenting deluge, mud, and muck causing John's work to slow even as he tried to hurry. Finally, he was able to slide the shovel next to the coffin's lid and attempt to pry the lid open. His first few attempts resulted in the shovel's blade slipping off the wet wood.

Eventually, his persistence paid off and he felt the shovel catch in between the coffin and the lid. Water continued to sluice down the walls of the pit, flooding the area where John stood prying the lid upwards. His hands, strong yet aching, slipped on the smooth wooden handle of the shovel with each thrust. Prying and pulling the lid upwards took all of his remaining energy, yet he continued.

The bell chimed again over his head. He looked up, desperation on his face, and to his horror, he saw it dancing gently on the thin rope. Had the wind rung it? Or was it still dear Annie, clawing and clamoring under his feet? John cried out at the thought, grabbed the twine, and gave it three distinct yet gentle tugs, to give the woman hope. He continued to pry the lid, pushing and heaving against the nails that were working against him. He felt them give a little and renewed his efforts.

It was then that he noticed the twine, once hanging straight yet loose, was being pulled taut. Once, twice, three times! Annie, oh dear Annie! John began laughing at the horror of the situation. Once he started laughing though, it kept coming, and John worried that he had indeed gone completely and utterly mad.

With his final laugh turning into a grunt, he felt the lid give way enough for him to get his fingers underneath the lid. He quickly fell to his knees in the thick mud of the pit and tried to see into the coffin.

"Annie! Are you okay?" he called out. He could see nothing in the wooden box except sheer darkness. The grave itself was pitch black at this point. He quickly stood up and climbed up just enough to grab the lantern's metal handle. Casting the dim light into the hole where he stood, he climbed back down to the coffin.

"Can you see the light?" he asked, holding the small flame close to the lifted wood planks of the lid. "I am here. I am trying to set you free." He listened but heard nothing except the wind and rain overhead. Quickly finding a level spot for the lantern he set it down so that he could continue his work.

With a few more yanks, the pine plank he was working on gave way completely, and John tore it from the coffin. Grabbing the lantern, he held it over the head of the coffin to see inside. He had to lean over slightly to get a glimpse into the shadows.

The smell that permeated the air now turned from that of dirt and mud to that of rot and decay. John pulled back immediately, covering his nose with his hand. The fetid stench surrounded him, swirling with the wind overhead. He swallowed the bile rising in his chest and bent to take another look.

There, below his feet, lay the earthly remains of Annie Flynn, skin marbled, face bloated and disfigured. Her arms appeared to still be crossed over her chest in the same position she'd been laid to rest in.

John was completely confused and his arms began to shake. Annie was most definitely dead. But if she was dead, who, or what, had rung the bell? That insane burial bell? John stood back from the maddening scene before him and looked around, for what he did not know.

The rain above him continued pouring over the edges of the grave, water accumulating around the coffin. But still, John stood there, chest heaving, mind whirling. What to do now, he wondered. He stood over the open coffin, staring down at its inhabitant.

Dead, decaying Annie Flynn.

A shiver ran down John's spine. He had thought he'd had a chance to save her but save her from what? She'd been dead for a few days, that much was apparent. But who had rung the bell? That damned burial bell? Surely it was the wind since Annie was unable to have done it.

Suddenly, bringing John out of his musing, the bell chimed yet again. Near hysteria, John glanced upward at the bell dancing on the twine, the twine yet again taut. Gulping, John slowly looked downward, the hairs on the back of his damp neck standing on end. His eyes slowly focused on Annie's cold, marbled face, her body motionless.

John started laughing hysterically, his mind playing tricks on him surely. But as he continued to stare at Annie's once beautiful face, John heard the bell once again, and to his horror, he saw Annie's eyes pop open and a hideous grin appeared on her face. In shock, John jumped backward but slipped in the mud, hitting his head on the shovel's edge on his way down.

The rain continued throughout that night, slowly eroding the edges of the grave and filling the pit with muddied water.

***

The next afternoon, a passerby stopped to visit St. Andrews Cemetery. What they saw in the grave that day forever changed the community. For at the bottom of the grave, in a plain pine box was the decaying corpse of Miss Annie Flynn, and sprawled atop her, another body.

That of John Sutton, the gravedigger, buried face down in the mud.

7

THE CAVERN

The hot July sun beat down on the trio of hikers as they meandered their way through an open patch of meadow. The sound of bees busily going about their day's work of pollination was accented by the heavy breathing exerted by the hikers' efforts. They were almost to the top of the rise, their clothes sticking to their sweat-covered bodies.

"There better be some shade soon. This sun....." Caleb commented, risking a glaring look up at the sun's unrelenting rays. The humidity was oppressive as well and Caleb worried about his asthma flaring up. He had his inhaler with him but was reluctant to use it, especially in front of Sarah.

He glanced over his shoulder now, watching Sarah as she made her way through the meadow of wildflowers behind him. She caught him watching her and smiled but he quickly turned back around, face red, and walked straight into Holden's back.

"Watch it, Caleb," Holden snapped, breathing heavily from exertion. Caleb mumbled his apologies but was grateful for the respite of walking uphill.

The trio had decided the night before to venture out on a day hike in the wilderness area in the nearby national forest; just one more item to mark off their "Summer of Fun Tour" before senior year started.

Caleb and Holden had been friends since the second grade and Caleb had mooned over Holden's twin sister, Sarah, the entire time. Caleb had never told Sarah of his feelings, unsure how to navigate through them. Holden would have just picked on him anyway and, unwilling to risk dismissal from Sarah, Caleb remained quiet, choosing to live in his own quiet prison of teenage angst and unrequited love.

"We're almost to the top. Looks like there are some trees up ahead," Holden pointed out with a nod. He removed the lid from his water bottle and took a greedy swig. "Lunch in the trees?"

"I'm game. I could use a break," Sarah agreed, taking a long drink from her water supply. Caleb nodded his consent to Holden as he, too, took a much-needed gulp of water from his orange water bottle.

"How much farther, do you think?" Sarah asked, casting a glance around her.

"I don't know. Mitch said the opening was like... two miles in?" Holden said, sliding off his backpack and fishing around in the contents. He pulled out a map of the area and, flipping it around, tried to make sense of it. "Let's get to the shade and see if we can figure out where we are."

The trio began their upward trek once again, Caleb feeling each step in his burning thighs. Usually, he'd be at home, sitting in the air conditioning while playing Xbox with his online friends. But then Holden had been talking with his older, and somewhat unreliable, cousin Mitch, about some hidden cave and missing hikers, and of course, Caleb's interest was piqued. It was all Holden would talk about for a week straight: going to see this damn cave. Caleb was apprehensive, to say the least. He'd never been spelunking or anything of the sort. He'd heard stories of people going into caves, getting lost or hurt, and never returning.

Mitch claimed that he knew where the opening to the hidden cave was. One that he said was shrouded in mystery. Caleb had rolled his eyes at the dramatic flare Mitch had added to his story but had listened anyway. Trying to act bored and disinterested, Caleb had listened to Mitch prattle on about missing hikers, strange happenings, and eerie sounds coming from the mysterious cave. Apparently, according to Mitch, the cave was so dangerous that the park rangers forbade anyone from going there, sealed off the opening, and removed it from all park maps. Caleb wondered how someone so air-headed as Mitch could have found something so interesting but he had kept his thoughts to himself. Caleb had been against this whole expedition until he heard Sarah was going. After that, he couldn't pack his daypack fast enough. Snacks, water, flashlight, extra batteries, more snacks. He even packed his K-Bar knife he'd gotten for his fifteenth birthday. He didn't know what he'd use it for but felt that it might be good to have along when descending into the unknown.

Now, the trio finally crested the hill and dropped their packs beneath a large oak tree. Sarah wiped her face with the hem of her tank top and Holden threw himself to the ground dramatically, breathing heavily from exertion. Caleb found himself leaning against the rough bark of the old oak, trying to catch his breath. After a few moments, heart rates calming, breathing back to normal, they all sat on the lumpy, root-gnarled ground and ate their lunch.

Caleb watched Sarah out of the corner of his eye as he ate his sandwich. She sat to his left, long, tanned legs crossed under her, chewing quietly on a peanut butter sandwich. Holden, on the other hand, was loudly chewing and talking about the plan to find the cave.

"If I'm looking at this right, and if Mitch marked the cave entrance correctly, we should be there in an hour or so," Holden exclaimed, a chunk of sandwich-laced spittle escaping his lips.

"But didn't Mitch say that the entrance was closed off?" Sarah asked, selecting a chip from the bag on her lap. "How does he even know this is the right cave? And why didn't he investigate it himself?"

Caleb nodded, noting these were all great questions. Probably questions they should have answered before marching into the wilderness alone and naive.

"He said he found a secret entrance. Duh," Holden ground out, rolling his eyes at his sister. "He didn't go inside because it was getting dark out."

"A secret entrance to a secret cave?" Sarah asked, her voice dripping with sarcasm. "Give me a break. Mitch is an idiot. And besides, a cave is dark regardless of whether the sun is out or not." Caleb had to agree. He just shrugged and continued eating.

"You know, Sarah, nobody made you tag along," Holden sniped, looking down his nose at his sister. "You were against it until I mentioned that Caleb was coming. You guys need to just kiss and get it over with." With that, Holden crammed the remnants of his lunch into his pack, stood, and stomped away towards the treeline nearby.

Caleb could feel his face heat and kept his eyes on the ground in front of him. He watched an ant crawl across his shoe but still didn't move. Holden knew? Holden knew Caleb had feelings for Sarah. He could feel her eyes on him now but he said nothing, moved nothing. Suddenly Sarah grabbed her lunch and stood.

"Holden! You're such an asshole!" she exclaimed as she went in search of her brother.

***

An hour or so later, the small group found themselves deep in the woods. The forest, dark except for random rays of sunlight penetrating the canopy above them, was quiet and dense. Holden, always in the lead, pressed onward with the GPS and map in hand. Caleb and Sarah followed behind, the drama at lunchtime forgotten for the moment.

"We should be there any minute according to this," Holden called over his shoulder, holding up his dad's old Garmin GPS. "Keep your eyes open for anything suspicious."

"Suspicious? Are we detectives now?" Sarah whispered from behind Caleb. Caleb turned to her and grinned, rolling his eyes in Holden's direction. Sarah giggled quietly and was about to whisper something else when Holden stopped short.

"There! That looks totally sus," Holden exclaimed, pointing to a rock outcropping a hundred yards or so ahead of them. There was a large crevasse between two large boulders. Holden loped ahead and peered inside. Caleb and Sarah ran after him to have a look.

It was just that— a crevasse— to nowhere. Holden let out a defeated sigh. "We should be there!"

"Maybe a crack in the wall is a cave to Mitch," Sarah offered sarcastically. Holden turned and glared at her.

"Maybe we just have to keep looking," Caleb shrugged, trying to diffuse the tension. "He said it was hidden, right? Let's just keep looking." He began walking around the rock face, looking for the cave entrance. Soon he heard someone come up next to him and found Sarah there, aiding in his search.

"Do you think we'll find anything, Caleb?" she asked quietly. He liked it when she said his name, her voice smooth like honey.

He shrugged, "Who knows?" At this point, he was just happy to be spending the day with her and didn't care if they ever found the cave.

After searching for fifteen minutes and finding nothing, the group was tired and disappointed. They had hiked out four miles or so in the summer heat to find what? Nothing. With a unified sigh, they sat down to regroup. Caleb leaned up against the hard rock face and picked up an acorn, rolling it around in his fingertips. Holden poured over the map, muttering to himself, while Sarah sat there looking around.

A few moments passed, the group sweating in the stagnant summer humidity. All of a sudden, Sarah squealed and stood up abruptly.

"Look! That plant just moved!" she exclaimed. The boys turned to see where she was pointing.

A few feet away from them, at the base of the rock, grew some bushy weeds with small purple flowers in them. The flowers were moving in the breeze.

"It's just some wildflowers in the breeze, Sarah," Holden sighed, seemingly annoyed at the sudden excitement.

"No! Look!" Sarah insisted, crawling over to the bush. "The flowers are moving, but there isn't a breeze."

Caleb and Holden felt for a breeze but felt nothing in the stagnant summer heat and yet the flowers continued to dance slightly, to and fro. Sarah, not waiting for the boys, began looking at the bush from all angles, pulling it this way and that.

"I can feel it! I can feel the breeze!" Sarah exclaimed excitedly as she began pulling at the bush. "There is something behind this bush. I can feel the coolness! I think I've found the cave!"

Together, the three teens tugged at the bush, ever desperate to reveal its secrets. Finally, the roots began to give way and the bush slowly relinquished its hold on the earth and ripped free. There, behind where the bush had been, was a small opening roughly three feet wide and two feet tall. A cool damp breeze flowed out of the abyss, cooling the energized hikers.

"The opening!" Holden exclaimed, already army-crawling to look inside. Caleb felt uneasy about the whole thing suddenly, but not wanting to appear weak to Sarah, remained quiet.

"Be careful, Holden," Sarah cautioned, squatting down to look in the hole. Holden muttered something sarcastic but kept belly-crawling forward. He was over halfway into the cave now with only his socks and tennis shoes still visible to the others.

"What do you see?" Caleb asked, interested yet apprehensive. By now, Holden was completely out of sight. Sarah and Caleb could hear nothing except for the normal forest sounds around them.

"Holden?" Sarah called into the abyss. She cast her flashlight beam about the interior of the hole but could see nothing. Caleb, down on his hands and knees next to her, could see nothing either. He could, however, hear Sarah's breathing near his ear and smell the shampoo in her hair from her shower that morning. He inhaled lightly, enjoying her closeness as their shoulders bumped, while they looked into the cave in front of them.

"Should we go after him?" Sarah asked, sounding worried as she turned to look at Caleb. He felt his heartbeat pick up as he looked into her face just mere inches from his own. "I can't hear him!" The desperation in her voice brought him out of his thoughts. Now was not the time for such thoughts anyway, he inwardly chastised himself.

"Holden! This isn't funny!" Caleb called into the hole. "Say something!"

He was met with silence.

"I'm going in," Sarah muttered, sticking her flashlight between her teeth and making a move to head into the cave. "Coming?" she asked, the word garbled.

Caleb nodded and the two of them proceeded to crawl into the opening. Caleb could feel the roof of the tunnel scraping at his day pack and tried not to think about all the rock that surrounded them. They could be entombed in this cave and no one would ever find them. He suddenly wished he'd told his mom more about what they were doing that day, but he'd chosen instead to be vague. She had no idea where he was.

"Hanging out with Holden," could mean anything. Cringing at his stupidity, but unwilling to leave Sarah, Caleb pressed on, gravel and sand crunching under his knees and hands.

Up ahead of him, he could see nothing but darkness and the vague outline of Sarah crawling on her knees and elbows which was fine with him. Anything to keep his mind off the fact that they were tunneling into unknown territory. The tunnel opened up slightly then, allowing for more shoulder space, but began to descend slowly. Caleb had thoughts of the tunnel suddenly disappearing and them free-falling to a certain death. He shook his head now at the thought.

"Do you see anything? Can you hear Holden?" he asked. Sarah said something but he couldn't discern it over the sound of the gravel crunching under their knees and hands. The darkness seemed to envelop them in its inky shadows and Caleb wondered what kind of creatures called this cave home. What if it opened up and there was a cougar or bear or something waiting to eat them? Or cave spiders? Weren't cave spiders a thing? He gulped as his thoughts ran rampant. Oh, how he wished he was at home on the Xbox!

"Stand up," came Sarah's voice. Caleb looked around, confused for a moment. It was then that he realized that

Sarah was standing in front of him. He had been so deep in thought that he hadn't noticed she'd stopped crawling. He awkwardly stood, narrowly missing hitting his head on the low ceiling. He took a moment to survey their surroundings.

"Where's Holden?" he asked, looking around at the chamber they were now in. The tunnel had opened up into a small room roughly twenty feet across and six feet or so high. On the other side of the stone room, Caleb could see two, maybe three, more passageways heading deeper underground.

"He's an idiot. Should have stayed here or come back for us," Sarah grumbled, annoyance on her face. "In pure Holden fashion, he's gone rogue."

"Want to look for him? Or wait for him outside?" Caleb asked. They had no idea where the passageways went and didn't even know which one Holden had taken.

"I don't know. He could get lost. Who knows how big this system is? I don't want to get lost looking for him," she sighed, looking around again with her flashlight. Caleb could think of a few things to pass the time with Sarah but kept them to himself. Who was he kidding? He didn't have the guts to even ask her out, much less try to make a move.

He moaned inwardly at himself and set about trying to determine which passageway Holden had gone down. The first one only went about six feet in and was empty when Caleb shined his light inside. He moved on to the second.

This tunnel appeared to be longer, the end too far away to be penetrated by the flashlight beam. Glancing at his feet, Caleb noticed a footprint in the sand; a Nike similar in size to Holden's.

"I think he went this way— " he began to say when suddenly there was a noise from the third tunnel. A slight scraping sound was followed by small rocks being scattered about. Caleb shined his light in the direction of the third passageway and Sarah quickly joined him.

"Holden?" Sarah called into the darkness, her flashlight doing little to illuminate the way. They were met with silence.

"I saw a shoe print over in that tunnel. I thought he went that way but now—" Caleb's voice trailed off. Suddenly they heard a low moaning sound coming from the passageway ahead of them.

"Holden, you asshole, get out here!" Sarah snapped, anger darkening her pretty face. Caleb noticed she was covered in dust and dirt but was as beautiful as ever, even if she was mad. Breaking through his thoughts, Sarah began heading down the third tunnel, where the sounds had come from. Caleb quietly followed.

They'd only gone about twenty yards or so when the passageway turned left and then a few yards further, diverged into three more passageways yet again. Shining their flashlights around the walls and ceiling of the cave, Caleb and Sarah saw no signs of Holden anywhere.

"He better not have gone down another passage. We're going to get lost for sure!" Sarah set her mouth in a grim line, her face a mix of annoyance and uncertainty. She was right though, Caleb concluded. With the tunnels and cave branching off of each other it would be easy to lose their way.

"If we are going to go any further, we should mark the tunnel somehow," Caleb suggested, having gotten the idea from a movie or book.

"I don't have any paint. Do you?" Sarah asked, slinging her backpack off her thin shoulders and unzipping it. "Let's see.....I have an ink pen. No good."

"I have a hoodie and an extra pair of socks. No good," Caleb sighed, beginning to feel frustrated. Where was Holden? If he hadn't run off they wouldn't be in this mess.

"Oh! I have this!" Sarah announced, holding up a stick of red lipstick. "It was in the bottom of my purse. Must have fallen out into my backpack."

"That would work! We can make X's on the walls when we go down tunnels," Caleb said, shining his light towards the opening they had just come from. Sarah grinned at Caleb and then skipped over to mark the wall.

"Since this was the farther right tunnel we came down, let's go down the farthest right one in this room too. That way, when we turn around we can just do left, left, left.... We still have to find Holden so who knows where we will end up," Sarah sighed, rolling her eyes. She was about to say something else but then paused, just standing there in front of Caleb.

"Are you okay? You look worried," she asked, looking up at Caleb's face. "We're going to find him and get out of this weird hole." She reached out then and gently placed her hand on Caleb's forearm, his breath instantly caught in his throat. "You good?" he heard her ask.

For reasons unknown to him, Caleb just stood there, looking down at Sarah's upturned face. He took in her blue eyes with their long lashes. The little sprinkle of freckles across her nose and cheeks. He even noticed the small scar on her forehead from a bicycle accident when they were ten.

Suddenly, emboldened somehow, Caleb felt himself slowly leaning into Sarah, his lips just inches from hers. He could feel her breath on his cheek, her eyes closing as she leaned into him. Just when their lips were about to make contact, laughter erupted from down another tunnel.

"Good grief, Caleb!" Holden laughed, appearing at the opening of the passage. "I leave you alone with my sister for two minutes and you're already trying to make out with her." He started cackling again then, holding his stomach as he bent over laughing dramatically.

Sarah and Caleb jumped apart, annoyed at Holden and his untimely reappearance.

"Grow up, Holden!" Sarah snapped. She stepped over to a nearby boulder and sat down with a sigh. "Where were you?" she demanded. "We've been calling for you and you just ran off."

"Chill, Sis," Holden sneered, "I have something to show you. Come this way." He turned around and began walking back down the passageway he'd just come from. Caleb and Sarah stood there for a second watching Holden's flashlight beam bounce around the passageway's surface and slowly disappear. With a sigh, the two followed him.

This passage was taller than the rest, possibly twelve feet high. Caleb couldn't be sure of the height but was happy that he no longer had to watch his head. The ground beneath them also seemed a little rougher, causing Sarah to stumble a few times. Caleb was there to catch her of course, while Holden led the way.

Downward the trio walked, the way rocky and uneven. Caleb began to worry again, and his anxiety spiked. He hated that about himself–always the worrier. He wanted to be brave for once. To not think about "what if?"

He was jarred out of his thoughts of self-recrimination when Holden spoke.

"Check it out, guys," Holden flashed his light ahead of them on the cavern floor. There appeared to be a large black expanse in front of them.

"Is that... water?" Caleb asked, stepping around Holden carefully and looking into the murky depths before him. It did indeed look to be an underground lake of some sort, depths unknown.

"Yep," Holden preened proudly, as though he deserved an award for finding such a discovery. "It's deeper than my arm. I tried sticking my arm in already. It's pretty cold."

"I bet. It's pretty chilly in here," Sarah commented as she looked into the rocked rimmed water in front of them. Without hesitation, Caleb shrugged off his day pack and pulled out his hoodie, handing it to Sarah. She took it with a smile and slid it over her head.

"It's not that cold, guys," Holden stated, sitting down on a large rock formation. He began untying his shoes and removing them. His socks followed.

"What are you doing?" Sarah asked sudden concern in her voice. "You can't seriously be thinking about going for a swim in that!"

"Don't be a wimp. It's just... refreshing," Holden scoffed, pulling his tee shirt over his head and stepping up to the edge of the dark pool. He stood there a moment, looking into its murky depths, and just as Caleb was about to voice his concerns about the stupidity of jumping into an unknown body of water, Holden hollered, "Cannon-ball!" and jumped feet-first into the chilly water.

Sarah and Caleb both hopped back a step to avoid the splash their friend had just made. Once the water had landed safely on the stone floor, they crept closer to the black pool, shining their flashlights in to look for Holden.

They didn't see him and eventually, the waves he had made slowly receded and the surface became calm again. Sarah moved her flashlight all around looking for even a glimpse of her brother yet saw nothing.

"Holden!" Caleb called, leaning over the dark, murky pool. "Holden! This isn't funny!"

Seconds passed but still, the missing teenager did not surface. Caleb began to panic, wondering if Holden was okay. They had no idea of the depths of the water, or what creatures may call it home. Caleb tried not to think about his freshman biology class and Mrs. Nelson talking about some creepy cavefish that didn't have any eyes or something. He hadn't been paying attention then, too busy doodling pictures of Spider-Man in his notebook. Now, as he leaned over the cavernous pool, he wished he'd paid more attention to Mrs. Nelson's lessons. Then maybe he'd know what they were up against.

"Holden! You piece of—" Sarah grumbled, down on her hands and knees, leaning over the lip of the rock. Just then, Holden splashed through the surface with a gasp from holding his breath for so long. When he saw Sarah and Caleb looking distraught, he grinned at them as he tread water, making no move to exit the pool.

"Guys, this is *so* cool!" he exclaimed, slicking his hair back out of his eyes. "I swam down pretty far and never even touched the bottom! What if this is some new discovery? Maybe they will call it Lake Holden after me." He laughed at himself then.

"Unlikely," Sarah muttered, half relieved, half glaring at her brother. "What took so long? You scared us."

"I just told you. I swam toward the bottom," Holden repeated, leaning back to float on his back. "It's pretty nice in here. Maybe you guys should try it. The coolness will chill you out."

"I'm not going in there," Sarah stated, crossing her arms across her chest. "I think you should get out. We need to get back home. It's getting late."

"Good grief, Sarah. Since when were you such a weenie? I knew we shouldn't have brought you along today. Right, Caleb?" Holden glared at his sister. "Oh, wait. You wouldn't have come either. Not if Sarah wasn't coming. Well, maybe next time I'll come alone and—" Holden stiffened up just then, his voice trailing off. His eyes grew large and he looked panicked. "Guys... there's something in here. Something in the water!"

"What? This better not be another one of your stupid jokes, Holden," Sarah snapped, standing to her feet and stepping back. Caleb stood beside her as they watched Holden flail in the murky depths of the pool.

"I'm not joking!" Holden yelled, his voice raising an octave as panic consumed him. "Something brushed against my leg! Something big!"

Caleb could tell by the look in Holden's eyes that he wasn't joking this time. Not even a little bit. He watched as his friend began thrashing at the water and desperately trying to swim to the rocky edge. The water sloshed out onto the stone lip of the pool, causing the surface to be slick but Caleb tried to lean out as far as he could anyway to reach Holden's outstretched hand.

"There's something in here with me!" Holden's pan-icked screams echoed off of the cavern walls. "Get me out! Get me out of here!"

Caleb's hand was mere inches away from Holden's when suddenly his friend disappeared under the surface for a second or two and then resurfaced, a scream erupting from his chest. "It's biting me! Oh my God! It's biting me!"

"What? Give me your hand!" Caleb yelled, leaning far-ther out over the water. He felt Sarah grab his other hand to help support him but he never took his eyes off of Hold-en's anguished face. Water and tears sluiced over Hold-en, snot streaming from his nose as he clutched madly at Caleb's hand.

"Ah! My leg! Something is biting me!" Holden screamed again, desperately smacking at the water in a frantic motion. Just then, when Caleb's hand began wrapping around Holden's cold, sodden one, something hidden be-neath the abysmal surface seemed to grab Holden and pull him roughly away from the edge towards the middle of the water. It was hard to see anything in the cavernous room, lit only by the three meager beams of light from the flashlights. Caleb cried out for Holden but heard nothing except the churning of water echoing on the limestone walls.

Suddenly, the water swirled and churned as something swam through it. Caleb's eyes sought out Holden as Sarah desperately moved the flashlight beam to and fro trying to illuminate the water. It was then, and only for a second, that Sarah and Caleb saw it. The creature that seemed to be tormenting their friend. Just a quick glimpse of scales, twisting and slipping through the darkened water. It was something large to be sure and suddenly Caleb wanted to be anywhere but there.

"Holden!" Caleb yelled, renewing his efforts to reach his friend but now trying to avoid falling into the pool himself. He and Sarah could hear nothing except the sound of churning water and their frantic screams. Where was Holden?

Just then, they heard a gasp as Holden broke the surface yet again, this time mere inches from the rock rim of the pool. He grasped the edge while frantically taking in deep gulps of air.

"Help me!" he cried, "Pull me out or I'm dead!"

Caleb and Sarah scurried into action, each taking hold of Holden's arms and pulling their limp friend from the water. With a final heave, the trio found themselves lying on the cold stone floor in the darkness of the cavern, just inches from the bottomless subterranean body of water. They stared at each other in horror, each trying to catch their breath, trying to understand what had just happened. It was then that their eyes traveled down Holden's legs and the nasty wounds there on each calf. Deep puncture wounds were open and bleeding from multiple places on his legs. Caleb scooted down farther to investigate the wounds and felt his stomach churn when he noticed bits of bone showing through the torn flesh. Dear God, what had gotten him? Surely not the eyeless fish Mrs. Nelson seemed so fond of.

"We have to get him out of here. Now!" Sarah grunted, trying desperately to pull her brother further from the water's edge. Holden let out a cry of pain that shook Caleb to his core.

There was so much blood. Would his friend even make it? *Think Caleb!* He racked his mind on what to do. Suddenly it came to him, an obscure lesson he'd learned in Boy Scouts when he was twelve.

"We need to apply a tourniquet," he instructed Sarah. He began unbuckling his belt and pulling it through the loops. "We can use this for one leg, but we need something for the other leg. You gotta belt?"

She shook her head as she watched him wrap his belt around Holden's left leg and pull it tight. He was rewarded for his efforts with a scream of pain from Holden.

"I have this," Sarah offered, pulling at the string of Caleb's hoodie she was wearing.

"It's not thick enough but it's better than nothing, I guess." He watched as she pulled it out of the hood and handed it to him. While he wrapped it around his friend's other leg, he could feel Sarah moving around the space but was too focused on the task at hand.

"Here."

He looked up and found her standing behind him, her back to the water. In her hand was her bra, a hot pink lacy number that, in a different scenario, Caleb would have enjoyed seeing, but the situation they were currently in was grave at best.

"Thanks. That will work," he accepted the garment and made quick work of wrapping it around Holden's leg and tying it tight.

"We need to go," Sarah sobbed, "He's going to die. There's too much bloo–"

Suddenly, and without warning, Sarah was yanked backward into the pool, her scream smothered by the water.

"Sarah!" Caleb cried out, lunging towards the lip of the pool where she'd just been standing. The water below churned and heaved, splashing over the rocky edge.

Despite searching relentlessly, his eyes ever moving, Caleb could see nothing in the inky abyss.

"Help her...," gasped Holden weakly, his eyes pleading for Caleb's help. Turning to glance at his friend for a second, then back to the thrashing water before him, Caleb had a decision to make.

He dove for his backpack and, dumping the contents, quickly found the Bowie knife he thought he'd never need. Without a second thought, he dove into the turbid water to find Sarah.

The icy liquid surrounded him, instantly taking his breath away, and causing him to push towards the surface for more air. He broke through the water, and for a moment, he caught a flash of Sarah's hand breaking the surface on the other side of the pool.

Shoving off toward her, he swiftly fought his way through the water when suddenly something large brushed up against him. Something smooth and scaly. Caleb pushed back at it with his leg as he swam toward the area where Sarah had just been.

Almost immediately he felt an intense pain coursing down his leg as what felt like millions of teeth tore through the flesh of his thigh. He let out a scream of agony, flailing at the water's surface. With the Bowie knife in hand, Caleb began blindly stabbing into the dark water surrounding him, hoping to God that he didn't accidentally stab himself or Sarah.

After a few thrusts of his knife just sliding through the water, he felt something brush against his leg again. Caleb stabbed through the dark waves again, feeling resistance. He'd hit something!

It was then that an otherworldly howl filled the cavern, echoing against the limestone walls. Caleb pulled the knife from his prey and continued to swim toward where he'd last seen Sarah.

The howling continued, almost to an ear-splitting level. Caleb tried to cover his ears while swimming but found it difficult. With effort, he finally made it to the far side of the pool and began searching for Sarah.

"Sarah!" he called, feeling around along the rocky edge, the surface cool to the touch. It was darker on this side, as the three flashlights were over with Holden. Everything Caleb could see was enshrouded in shadow. *Where was Sarah? Had she drowned? Had that creature succeeded in pulling her down to a watery grave?* He felt panic rising in his chest but still he pressed on.

The sound of the painful wails and howls continued as Caleb tried climbing out of the pool to get to a better vantage point. The wound in his leg proved to be too deep, causing too much bleeding and instability for him to climb.

With a grunt, he slipped on the bank of the pool and slid back into the dark water. Filled with frustration and agony, he let out a feral scream of his own. Taking a large gulp of air, he quickly dove under the dark surface, looking for Sarah. At the very least, he'd find whatever it was that had attacked them.

Suddenly all was silent, the water was calm again, but under the surface, a battle raged. Caleb found himself surrounded by churning water, darkness, and something evil.

Something hungry.

His lungs screamed for fresh air as he reached blindly around him, searching for any signs of Sarah. Something solid bumped into him from behind and then from the front, and just as he was about to give up and race to the surface for more air, he felt Sarah's hair, and then a wrist.

Grasping it firmly, he pulled her to the surface, desperate to get her to shore. But when he broke through the water, the dim light from the trio of flashlights on the distant edge of the pool revealed a new horror to Caleb.

For it wasn't Sarah that he'd pulled to the surface, but a beautiful siren, her long hair flowing out behind her. She watched the look on Caleb's face, her eyes laughing at him.

"Who are you?" Caleb demanded, "Where is Sarah?" He pulled the siren's arm, dragging her towards him. "Where is Sarah?"

"Stupid boy, you should have never come here," the creature said, her voice sultry and seductive. She pulled her arm from his grasp easily enough, seeming to cast a spell on him, as he tread water in the middle of the pool. "Don't you see? We are the sirens of this cave, and you are now dinner. Everyone who dares to enter this cavern, or wander too close to this pool becomes a meal." A sinister grin spread across her face and she let out a dark hiss of a laugh.

It was then that her face transformed from an almost human-looking woman to her true form—a scaly horrifying creature with razor-sharp teeth and gills. Where her hair had been only moments before, there were now strange tentacles.

Caleb screamed in horror at the terrifying scene before him and thrust himself backward into the water. It was then that he realized there was more than one siren, for in that moment, they all lunged at him and the last thing he saw coming at him were their razor-sharp teeth.

8

THE ANIMAL WITHIN

He was dead. That much was evident. His broken, bloodied body was crushed, a mess of fur and flesh. His pupils were fixed and dilated and his long tongue hung from his mouth, limp and turning blue as I watched. I sighed, my heart sinking. This is the part of my job I don't like. Having my patients die before I even have a chance to help. Having to tell their owners that their dogs are gone, lost forever.

It all started about twenty minutes or so after the last staff member left for the day. The receptionist, Shirley, was always the last to leave the animal hospital each night. Sometimes, I would leave with the staff, but usually, I was too busy finishing up with charts or calling owners to go over blood results. As a veterinarian, sometimes the job was exhausting and grueling and other times it was rewarding and exhilarating. Today had been one of the exhausting, grueling days. No time for lunch, just a quick protein bar and a swig of tepid coffee left over from the morning rush.

The day had started okay. A few routine surgeries, a hospitalized cat with a urinary obstruction, and a newly diagnosed diabetic. Mrs. Tendly called three times because her little chihuahua, Pico, sneezed twice. A technician called in sick, leaving the rest of the staff short-handed. Just a normal day in veterinary medicine.

Things began going south after the afternoon appointments started. There were two euthanasias, almost back to back. A Great Dane named Aries that I'd taken care of since puppyhood. The other was a new client with a large mixed breed with a splenic mass. Some appointments went longer than anticipated and we worked in two emergencies. Needless to say, by the time six o'clock rolled around, the staff and I were exhausted and ready to get home.

Shirley had left a few minutes after everyone else and I went to work filling out paperwork and writing up charts. The clinic was quiet, almost eerily so. I turned on some music to softly play in the background while I finished my work. I was so engrossed in my task that at first, I didn't hear the knocking on the front door. When the knocking began on the side door and turned to pounding I got up to look out the peephole. Before I could even get to the door, it burst open and a man pushed his way in, carrying a bloody, limp dog in his arms. I jumped back in surprise at the intrusion, silently cursing Shirley for not locking the door behind her when she left.

"You the doc?" the man demanded, lifting the dog closer to him. I nodded and pointed for him to lay the dog on the treatment table.

"What happened?" I asked, assessing the large shepherd for signs of life. His eyes were staring blindly and his gums were pale. I grabbed my stethoscope to listen.

"Hit by a car. Fucking neighbor," the man said with a huff. "He didn't even stop! He's going to pay for this." He sighed and ran his bloodied fingers through his hair as I listened for a heartbeat. I finally found it, weak and thready.

I wheeled the anesthesia machine over to the table and hooked up the oxygen for the dog to inhale. His breathing was shallow and blood trickled from his nostrils. I had barely turned the oxygen on and hooked up the monitoring equipment when the dog suddenly got stiff, vocalized a low wail, and then died. His tongue turned a horrible bluish-gray color almost instantly.

"What's happening? You have to save him!" the man half shouted, panic raising in his voice. Quickly starting CPR, I willed the dog to live, to come back to us. After a few agonizing moments, I listened again with my stethoscope but heard nothing. I looked from the dog to the man and slowly shook my head. The man's face contorted into one of pain and agony, and a sob escaped his throat.

"I'm so sorry. There just wasn't anything we could do," I explained, my spirits sinking. I felt horrible for the dog and the weeping man in front of me. Sobbing sounds broke from the man's chest and I handed him a box of tissues.

"I'll give you some time," I offered quietly and then retreated to the reception area to give the man some time to compose himself.

While listening to the man's muffled sobs in the treatment room, I tried to focus on writing in my other patients' charts. My head swam, my heart hurt. I was exhausted–mentally and physically. Although I didn't want to rush the man currently mourning over his battered pet, I was anxious for him to leave. I wanted to get home, and tend to my dogs who were probably wanting to go out to pee and eat their supper.

With a sigh, I began writing in a chart again while sitting in a chair in the reception area. I worked for a few moments, focusing on the task at hand. I was so deep in thought that I didn't even hear the man come up behind me until the floor squeaked under his worn-out gym shoes. With a start, I jumped and whirled around to look at the crying man.

Except he wasn't crying anymore. He was glaring at me, a look of hatred and aggression etched into his features. Almost before I could react, he lunged at me, his balled fist making contact with my mandible and jarring my teeth. What was happening? My mind raced, frantic to escape this situation, my body instantly in full "flight or fight" mode.

I fell sideways in my chair as his other fist came down on my person in quick succession to the first. Holding up my arms and trying to fend off my attacker, I slid to the floor to escape. I yelled for help, even though I knew no one would hear my pleas. The control panel for the security alarm was in the other room near the side door.

"You stupid piece of shit!" the man roared at me. "You didn't even try to save him!"

"He was already too far gone!" I tried explaining, covering my head to absorb the blows from the man's fists. I got up on my feet and, bowed over, tried to run. Suddenly I felt his foot make contact with my abdomen and I gasped. The pain shot through me and I couldn't breathe for a moment or two. Tears welled up in my eyes as I struggled to breathe, to escape this plight. I could taste blood in my mouth, warm and metallic.

"If you were a real doctor you would have saved him," the man spat in my face. I watched as he turned suddenly and retreated into the treatment room. Sitting up, I gasped for breath and slowly made it to my feet, my head swimming, my face hurting.

I was halfway to the front door, to freedom, when I felt him come up behind me with something in his hand. Then everything went black.

***

I woke up with a start, my eyes going in and out of focus. Unsure how long I was passed out, I tried to sit up, to look around and assess my surroundings. My head pounded, my body ached. I slowly sat up and found myself sitting on the X-ray table in the dark, the radiology door shut.

Was I alone? Was the man with the dead dog still in the building? Why was I in the X-ray room? I had so many questions swirling around in my muddled thoughts. With a soft groan, I reached up and felt the back of my head, and then looked at the dried blood on my hand. What had he hit me with?

I quickly checked my pockets for my cell phone but found nothing. Then I remembered turning on Pandora and leaving the phone next to the computer in the treatment room. I needed to call for help, needed to make it to a phone.

Quietly, yet awkwardly, getting to my feet, I crept over to the radiology door and turned the knob slowly. Peering out of the cracked door, I could see the lights had been turned off everywhere except the treatment room. I slowly opened the door further to peer out and listen for signs of the horrible man.

At first, I heard nothing and then the faintest sound reached my ears. Metal scraping on metal. The sound emanated from the treatment room and I quietly tip-toed down the hallway towards the sound. My mind was telling me to run but I knew that the three exits to the hospital were all visible from the treatment room. The back door was the nearest exit but also the most noticeable one for anyone in the treatment room.

The metal scraping sound came again, louder this time. I heard a human grunt and then a distinct groan of metal being pried apart. What was the man doing? Why didn't he just leave? Take his dead dog and leave?

I continued to creep down the hallway and stopped just outside the treatment room door. Carefully, slowly, I moved to look through the small space in between the door jamb and hinges. The man had pried open the drug safe with a crowbar. All of the controlled drugs used for anesthesia, sedation, or pain were scattered around the countertops. The man was pouring the pills and capsules into a cloth grocery bag hanging on his arm while pilfering around in a drawer for syringes.

This monster was stealing all the drugs!

Had that been his whole plan from the beginning? To barge in here, attack me, only to steal my drugs? And then it hit me with a start. Had he injured and killed his dog in some sick and twisted plot to gain entry to the hospital after hours? Suddenly, I was angry. This was my hospital, my DEA number, my drugs, and even my license to practice veterinary medicine that was at stake. Who did this man think he was?

I decided to make a run for the side door, to escape and call the police, but before I could even get halfway to the door, I felt the man tackle me. We fell to the floor in a heap of punching and kicking flesh. I fought with all I had, desperate to get away from this madman. I swung a fist at him, making contact with his jaw and jarring him back. Taking that small reprieve from attack, I stumbled up and made my way towards the door yet again but was quickly tripped when the man grabbed my ankle and pulled me to the floor.

"Not so fast, Doc," he sneered, holding my ankle in his iron grip. "I just came for the drugs, but I'm sure you figured that out by now." I continued to tug my leg free and even kick out with my free foot but only kicked air.

"Look, just take the damn drugs," I snapped, still fighting to free myself. I would call the police as soon as I could and file a report. It wasn't worth me losing my life to this madman over a few bottles of ketamine or morphine. "Just take them and go."

"I want the cash box, too," the man glared at me as he pulled me to my feet. He stood there in the lab, his large hands encircling my wrists in a tight grip. The sound of our heavy breathing filled the air as we sized each other up. Surely I could take him down, right?

Just then, there was the sound of a car door slamming somewhere outside and the man glanced at the front of the clinic. Taking my chance at him being distracted, I lunged at him, shoving him off balance to flee.

But to my utter horror, that was when everything went from bad to worse. He didn't just fall off balance.

He fell backward into the lab equipment, hitting his head on the microscope and then the sharp corner of the countertop before finally sliding to the floor. Blood flowed freely from a large gash on his forehead, his nose broken.

I stood there, stunned and immobile, staring at him for a moment as he lay there unmoving. I couldn't even see the rise and fall of his chest. The puddle of blood around his head was slowly getting bigger, creeping towards my feet in an ever-widening circle.

"Dear God, what have I done..." I whispered hoarsely to myself, as suddenly my brain seemed to log back into gear. I had to do something! Call for help, render aid, anything but stand there staring.

Quickly springing to action, I raced to the man's side to feel for a pulse. After multiple attempts, my hands began to shake as reality set in.

The man was dead.

Trying not to panic, I began frantically pacing, my mind all over the place. What should I do? Would the police even believe me? Surely not. They'd say I killed him in a rage because he was trying to steal from me. I'd lose everything: my family, my hospital, my license... my respect.

I had no proof. There weren't any security cameras in the hospital, despite my office manager's nagging that we should get them.

There were no witnesses. Everyone was gone for the day, the blinds closed. I couldn't think of any way to prove that it had been an accident, or that he'd attacked me first.

My hands began to sweat, and my pulse increased, but still, I paced, deep in thought. If I didn't tell the cops, then what should I do? I couldn't very well leave a dead guy lying in a puddle of his blood for the staff to find the next morning, now could I?

I had to get rid of the man's body. It was the only way. But how? I walked over to one of the exam room windows and peered out. The sun was dipping low in the western sky, painting it in shades of oranges and pinks. It was still too light out to risk dragging a corpse out of the building and across the parking lot. But even if I got him to my car, where would I take him then? It's not like I could store him in my garage freezer.

That's when it came to me. The perfect way for me to dispose of his body where no one would suspect a thing.

"Oh, God, how low I have sunk. Have mercy on my soul for what I am about to do," I prayed silently, even as my brain raced to finish the idea that had started growing there.

Slowly, I stepped around the corpse and made my way to the kennel area, where our chest freezer was stored for deceased pets. They were kept there, waiting for the crematory to come and retrieve them postmortem.

Was I really about to do this? I gulped, my head feeling dizzy at the mere thought. But then I thought of my wife and kids at home waiting on me. If I lost my license over this whole situation, we'd lose everything. This hospital, which I'd built from the ground up, was to be our retirement. My family was relying on me to keep it running smoothly. I had to do this.

With a sigh of resolve, I knew what must be done. I straightened my shoulders, stood tall, and began collecting supplies for the grisly task I was about to perform.

A new prick of fear stabbed down my back when I remembered that I still hadn't locked the side door— the same unlocked door that had started this whole nightmare.

I quickly slid through the treatment room, flipping off lights as I went. Once I'd locked the side door to the clinic, I quickly checked the other doors— couldn't have a replay of what had already happened, could we?

When I felt that everything was as secure as possible, the hospital dark, and unassuming to anyone passing by on the street, I began my macabre work. The only light I'd allowed myself was in the dental area that housed a stainless steel tub covered by a grate that we used for dental cleanings or random treatments involving water. The windowless room was perfect for keeping what I was about to do from prying eyes.

Swiftly donning an apron and heading back to the lab where the dead man lay, I used a plastic trash bag to wrap his bloodied head to reduce the amount of mess I'd inevitably have to clean up. Once his crushed skull was contained, I grabbed the man by the ankles and slowly pulled his dead weight down the short hallway to the dental sink.

Now the hard work would begin.

With much effort and some cursing, I was eventually able to pull his limp form onto the grate of the table. Out of breath, I paused to gather my thoughts before proceeding.

Unable to push off the inevitable any longer, I opened the narrow drawer that held the sharpened knife that I usually kept only for necropsy or sending animal heads to the lab for rabies testing. Thankfully clients didn't ask for an autopsy of their pets often, but in the event I was to perform one, I was prepared.

Taking the yellow-handled blade in hand, I began cutting. I started at the apex of his left arm. Cutting through the flesh of his shoulder proved to be harrowing work but before long, the flesh and tendons gave way revealing the white bone of the shoulder joint. With some manipulation, I was eventually able to disarticulate the arm from the body. Placing it into a waiting trash bag at my feet, I then moved to the other arm and repeated the process.

The man had been wearing a tee shirt with the sleeves ripped out, which had served me well before, but as I moved lower to begin working on his legs I came across the obstacle of his shorts.

Sighing, I used a pair of bandage scissors and quickly sliced through the dead man's shorts, exposing his legs and underwear. He was a tighty-whitey type of fellow and that was fine with me. I moved on.

I was sweating by the time I removed both legs at the hip and then separated them at the knees to reduce their size. Bagging them up with the arms, I took a deep breath. Now for the hardest part.

I could do this. I'd done it before on dogs and cats. It didn't mean I liked doing it, but I knew I could.

When an animal bites a human and has no record of a rabies vaccine, it must be quarantined or euthanized and their brain tissue sent to the state lab for rabies testing. This, of course, involves decapitating the animal. No veterinarian enjoys doing this.

Now, as I stood over the armless, legless dead man on my dental table, I let out a long sigh and began.

Before long, I was holding something I never thought I would: a severed human head.

Surely, I was going to Hell for this.

Trying not to let the encroaching feeling of panic seep into my veins, I kept working. The man's torso was still too large for what I had planned, so I continued working.

What seemed like hours later, I was finally finished. The man's body parts were safely hidden where no one would ever find them, stitched securely into the carcasses of the euthanized dogs that were to be picked up for cremation the next morning. The man's own dog had become a vessel of grim transport for my dark deeds.

Luckily for me, they were all communal cremations. Each one would be lit aflame, each cadaver bag unopened, my secret kept. If one were opened, it would appear as though the pet had had a necropsy performed.

As I cleaned up my mess, making sure to remove any traces of blood or tissue, I grinned to myself. Maybe everything would be okay after all. I wouldn't go to prison. I wouldn't lose my license. I wouldn't lose my standing in the community.

I was dumping the last of the bloody mop water down the drain when there was a knock at the side door. Jolting in terror, I froze, willing the person to go away. Who would be knocking on the door at 11 pm?

The knocking persisted, getting more intense, and I began to panic. Had anyone seen something? Did they know about the man I'd just butchered?

I quietly crept to the door and peered through the hole. It was the police!

"Police! Doc, are you in there?" the officer called as he raised his hand to knock again. He wasn't going to leave. I noticed belatedly that I'd forgotten and turned the treatment room light back on while I cleaned up, leaving no doubt that someone was in the hospital. *Idiot*, I silently chastised myself.

Taking a deep breath to settle my nerves, I plastered on a smile and opened the door.

"Ah, Officer Hendricks!" I greeted cheerily. I needed to tone it down... it was too much. "What brings you here so late?"

"I was going to ask you that, Doc. Everything okay?" Hendricks asked, glancing over my shoulder.

"Yeah, yeah. Helluva day," I shrugged. "I was writing up charts and I must have dozed off."

"Oh, okay. I was just driving by and noticed your car parked out here and the light on inside. Just thought I'd check on you," Hendricks offered. "You heard about Dr. Whellon over in Cedarville, right? Got stabbed by some junkie looking for drugs. She's okay though, but still. Make sure you keep the doors locked when you're here late."

"Oh, no, I hadn't heard about Janine. Do they know who stabbed her?" I asked, my mind racing.

"Nah. Security camera just showed a man rushing into the clinic after hours with a hurt dog and then the guy attacked her. He used the dog as a way to gain entrance inside. She said he attacked her, then pried open the safe, and took all the drugs. Luckily for her, she had her cell phone in her pocket and was able to call 911 before she passed out."

"Wow.... How horrible!" I lamented. I was at a loss for words. So my suspicions had been true about the man after all. He *had* used the dog to get the drugs. He just hadn't meant to fall and die from a head wound.

"Tell me about it," Hendricks nodded. "Well, hey man, don't let me keep you. Just wanted to check on you."

"Sure, any time. Thanks, Officer," I said, watching as he turned and headed back toward his cruiser. As I was turning to close the hospital door behind me quickly, he called my name. My blood chilled as I turned to look at him.

"Oh, hey, you might want a new shirt, Doc. That's a lot of blood. Hope the patient made it." With a shrug, he got in the cruiser and drove away.

It was then that I looked down at myself, and there all across the front of my shirt was smeared blood. Not from a patient, but from a different kind of animal.

9

LITTLE JAR OF TEETH

The events of the past few weeks have been strange for me. Insane even. I'm sure anyone who moves three states over could say that though. Picking up your life, transporting all your things, your livelihood, to somewhere completely different... Except this time, for me, it *was* different. Something wasn't right about the new house, or the new town. Something seemed off.

Something sinister.

Six weeks ago, I decided to take a job a few states away. This involved a lot of logistical juggling, trying to find a new place to live while selling the old house. Lucky for me, my friend Stacey is a realtor, and my old home on Maple Street was sold within two days of listing it. A professor and her husband were thrilled to be moving in, especially since it was so close to campus.

I wasn't so lucky trying to find a new house though. The only realtor in the small town of Kellner was a musty old storefront crammed between the post office and hair salon.

I remember the day I moved to that town like it was yesterday. I remember everything that happened during my stay there.

The rain had just started coming down in sheets as I pulled up outside the small realtor's office and inwardly sighed. Today was signing day. I hated paperwork and just wanted to get on with it. I'd looked at the two houses available for sale in Kellner and eventually had decided on the pale yellow cottage near the edge of town.

After sitting in the car for a few moments, willing the rain to let up but soon realizing it wasn't going to, I finally just made a run for it. A squeal escaped my lips as the cold rain pelted me from all directions. Quickly slamming the car door, I ran across the sidewalk, ripping open the door to the realty office and letting it close behind me.

"Ah! Miss Sullivan!" Mr. Boyd greeted me, looking up as I stood dripping rainwater on his doormat. "You made it! Are you ready to buy a house today?" A grin spread across his wrinkly face, revealing an uneven row of cof-fee-stained teeth.

"Yes, sir," I nodded, sure he used that line with everyone on signing day. "I just want to get the paperwork done and get moved in. I stayed in a hotel last night and can't wait to get set up in my new home tonight, you know?"

"Oh, I understand, Miss Sullivan," he nodded, rotating to pull a stack of paperwork from an old beat-up filing cabinet behind his desk. "Hopefully the rain lets up for you. Got anybody helping you unpack?"

"No, but I don't have much," I informed the realtor, taking a seat opposite him and selecting an ink pen from a ceramic mug with a crack down the side. It was times like this that I was glad I was somewhat of a minimalist. The bonus for me was that the house came partially furnished.

"That's good, that's good," Mr. Boyd smiled at me before taking a loud, slurpy swig of his coffee. "The bed and kitchen table will help, I'm sure."

I nodded in agreement, even though I had every intention of purchasing a new mattress as soon as possible. From what I'd been told, the house had sat empty for a few years, the owner's adult children coming through every so often to check for leaks in the roof or unwanted tenants–both the human and the animal kind. The elderly owner had been living in a care home somewhere but the living will had some clause stating that the house wasn't to be sold until the owner's death. The old man had recently died and I reaped the benefits. His children wanted nothing to do with the house and were selling it as-is for cheap which is why I snatched it up—that and the fact that it was so close to the sea.

Just the thought of the sea, crashing into the rocks below the house, swirling and foaming, made me smile; the salt in the air, the sound of the gulls, the bells clanging off in the distance.

"Okay, Miss Sullivan, I need you to sign here," Mr. Boyd's voice brought my thoughts back to the task at hand and I glanced down at a highlighted "X" at the bottom of a page full of legal jargon. "And here." He flipped to the next page.

And so it went for what felt like three hours.

When we were finally done and my left hand was cramping from signing my name so many times, Mr. Boyd finally sat back in his seat.

"Welcome to Kellner, neighbor!" he beamed, his jagged coffee-stained smile making another appearance. He stood abruptly and leaned across his desk, jutting his hand out to me. Though I hate handshakes, I swallowed my distaste, plastered on a smile, and pumped his hand.

"Thank you, Mr. Boyd. It's so exciting to be a part of this town," I exclaimed, genuinely excited for the prospects of a new beginning.

After a blessedly short limp-wristed handshake, Mr. Boyd let go of my hand to yank open a desk drawer and rummage around. Pulling out a set of keys, he handed them over to me.

"Here you go, Miss Sullivan. This one is the front door, there's one for the back door, and this one must be the cellar. Maybe the shed?" he shrugged. "You'll just have to play around with them and figure it out I guess."

I nodded and accepted the keys and a copy of my mortgage paperwork before heading out to my vehicle. Waving goodbye to Mr. Boyd, I left the realty office, glad to see that the rain had finally let up. Maybe the day would turn out to be nice after all.

Ten minutes later I pulled into the driveway of my new home. The cottage, painted a soft yellow, had white gingerbread trim and a light blue door. A glassed-in three-season room hung off the back of the house, facing the sea. I couldn't wait to spend time out there reading. Maybe I'd get a cat, an orange, fat one, to sit on my lap.

I sighed contentedly, just thinking about all of the possibilities. With a grin, I parked the car, grabbed a box, and made my way up to the front door. Slipping the key into the lock and turning the knob, the blue door gave way with a soft creak from disuse, and I stepped into my new home.

The house was quiet and dusty, with cobwebs dangling from the light fixtures. I knew there would be cleaning involved before I moved all of my things in as the house had sat empty, but suddenly I was exhausted. *Maybe I could clean just one room, enough to move in the things I'd need immediately, and then take a nap?* I mused to myself.

I decided to start with the living room since it was right in front of me. There were two pieces of furniture, covered in sheets, in the middle of the room: an ugly couch and chair set from the 70s that I'd seen when I did the walkthrough with Mr. Boyd. I would be replacing them immediately, but first, I needed some floor cleaner, a mop, a rag, and a broom. Having some of the items in my car, but being too lazy to go dig around out there, I decided to try my luck in the kitchen.

Making my way to the kitchen, my feet made sticky sounds on the old black and white checked linoleum. I let out a sigh, remembering again that I'd be replacing the flooring in the kitchen soon too. I had so much work ahead of me. *Maybe I should have just rented*, I thought as I bent down to poke around under the kitchen sink.

I was in luck! There was a partial bottle of Mr. Clean and a small bucket, not to mention some mouse droppings, under there. Maybe I really should get a cat.

Sticking the bucket in the sink and turning on the tap, I prayed that the well would work fine. It had when we did the walkthrough but if something happened to it now, I wouldn't have a clue what to do as it was my first time with a well.

After a few seconds of coughing and wheezing, water eventually came pouring out of the old faucet and into the bucket. A victorious smile crossed my face and some of the tension left my shoulders.

Leaving the bucket to fill, I turned to check the pantry closet for a mop or broom and again, found exactly what I needed. Suddenly invigorated, my need for a nap momentarily forgotten, I grabbed the cleaning items and headed to the living room to get started.

***

By nightfall, I had thoroughly cleaned the living room, dining room, bathroom, bedroom, and half of the kitchen. I was exhausted! Pausing only to eat a peanut butter sandwich and potato chips for dinner, I'd spent most of the day hard at work. The next day I planned on finishing the kitchen, laundry, three-season room, and the guest room. I'd leave the creepy basement until I desperately had to.

I'd gone down there with Mr. Boyd during the walk-through, long enough to see that, yep, there was indeed a working hot water tank and furnace. But the amount of spiderwebs, the dirt floor, and the musty, earthy smell were enough to make me want to never venture down there again. I shiver every time I think about it.

Finally slipping into bed around midnight, I fell asleep almost instantly. Despite having to cover the questionable cleanliness of the current mattress with an extra blanket I'd brought with me, I was strangely comfortable.

It was somewhere in the wee hours of the morning, the sky still dark, when something awoke me. Disoriented, I sat up in bed and rubbed my eyes, trying to see anything in the shadows of my room. What woke me up?

After sitting silently on the bed for a moment, in a sleep-induced haze, I finally decided to get up, check the house, and grab a drink before trying to fall back asleep. I quickly made my way through the small cottage, checking the window locks and the doors again before getting a glass of water from the fridge. Taking a few sips, I set it on the counter and then quietly padded back to bed.

I'd only just laid back down and begun to relax when I heard a sound. It sounded like... gnawing. Like teeth being ground together. It was such a quiet sound at first, I almost didn't even hear it, but then it seemed to grow in intensity. *Damn mouse! No, rats!* I thought. *I better not have rats!*

The thought of rats lurking around my house, scurrying in the walls, made my flesh crawl. Their beady eyes, their long, hairless tails...

I sat back up in bed, my heart beginning to pound erratically as my thoughts ran wild. My mother always told me I had an overactive imagination and now I could see why.

The gnawing sound continued, but I couldn't tell where it was coming from. Was I imagining it? Maybe there *were* rats in the walls?

Sitting in the darkness, the blanket tucked up under my armpits, I turned my head this way and that trying to discern the origin of the sound.

Suddenly, there was a flash of lightning, and the room illuminated for a moment. I didn't see anything disturbing, like a rodent. Once the rumbling sound of the thunder rolled away, I strained my ears to listen for the gnawing sound but found that it had been replaced by the patter of rain on the old slate tiles of the cottage's roof.

With a sigh and a yawn, I lay back down, exhaustion soon consuming me once again. Maybe I had imagined the chewing sounds after all.

***

The next morning dawned warm and humid, the air still damp from the late-night storm. I woke with renewed vigor, despite being awakened by the creepy gnawing sounds just a few hours before, and quickly set about making coffee and preparing for my day.

I'd purposely made sure to give myself a solid two weeks for unpacking and getting to know my new little seaside town before reporting to work at Claremont Industries, where I would be a project manager. Luckily for me, the job was to be hybrid: two days in the office, three days working from home for the first few months, and then down to one day in the office. I was excited to work from home, and by home, I meant my enclosed porch overlooking the sea.

Taking my coffee out to the porch now, I slowly surveyed my new work area. I was happy to find that the porch wasn't just screened in as I'd first thought but was made up of windows. This was great news as I'd be able to work out there longer into the year, even after the weather had turned cooler.

I pulled out my phone and added "space heater" to my ever-growing list of things to get for the house. It was only September, but I knew cooler weather was around the corner, especially on the coast, so I'd have to get one sooner rather than later.

Deciding to tackle the porch first, I set about pulling the old wicker glider and chair out of the way so that I could sweep and mop. I used the broom to clear the ceiling and fan free of cobwebs and dust bunnies.

I was clearing out the corner of the porch that butted up against the house when I bumped my elbow on a small table sitting there. Casting an irritated glance into the grimy mirror on the wall over the table, I rubbed my bruised arm, while checking out the table. Something about it looked strange; I couldn't figure it out at first. As soon as I lifted the lid though, a smile crept across my face. It wasn't a table after all, but a record player.

Not knowing if it worked, or if there were any records left in the house, I decided to look around. I bent down to look on the shelf under the table and saw a dusty Janis Joplin record and a single from some band I'd never heard of.

Standing up, I let out a squeal, for there, in the reflection of the mirror over the table, was someone watching me! A young woman stood on the porch just inside the door leading to the backyard. Her long dark hair hung down, obscuring most of her face as she stood there wearing jeans and a grimy red and white tee shirt. I gasped, whipping around in shock that I suddenly wasn't alone. I hadn't even heard her come inside.

But there was no one there.

What the hell had just happened? Nope. This wasn't happening. I dropped the broom and ran back inside the house, slamming the door behind me. Clicking the lock into place, I slid down the back door, breathing hard. Who was that? Where had she come from? And more importantly, where did she go?

I rubbed my sweaty palms on my thighs, trying to think of what to do next. Surely I was being ridiculous... right? Part of my brain told me that as soon as I stood up and looked out of the window, the girl would be on the other side, peering in at me, all creepy-like. As I mentioned before, Mom always said I had a crazy imagination.

She wasn't wrong.

It was probably also the same reason I was dreaming about rats chewing through my walls last night, too.

With an embarrassed sigh, I decided to quit acting like a two-year-old and stood up. Turning to look back out on the porch, I was secretly relieved to see that it was empty.

Suddenly, a loud pounding at the front door had me all but climbing the walls. I covered my mouth with my hand to muffle my scream. My heart felt like it was going to beat out of my chest. Who was here? Was it the creepy girl that had just been on my porch?

The pounding continued, more of a knocking sound if I'm being honest. I had to answer it. I had to prove to myself that the girl was real and I was just an idiot.

I quickly went to the front door and, before I lost my nerve, whipped it open. It was only after I'd opened the door widely that I remembered I was still in my sleep shorts and tank top, hair a mess.

The person on the porch was most definitely not the creepy porch girl. He was tall, well-muscled, and lean. His dark hair was perfectly messy and fell over his dark blue eyes.

Whoever he was, he was hot... and I looked like a train-wreck, all sweaty and freaked out over a creepy girl on my porch.

"Hi, I'm Evan. I live next door," he greeted me, his eyes taking in my appearance. "I saw you were moving in and thought I'd come introduce myself, and see if you needed any help with anything."

"Oh..." I stammered, still flustered by the girl. "I'm Hailey. And hey, since you're here.... You didn't happen to see a girl walking around my yard just now did you?"

Evan gave me a confused look, "No, I haven't seen anyone. Just you. This is the last house on the point here, kinda secluded, you know?"

I nodded, looking around. He was correct about that. My cottage was the last one on the lane before it narrowed and wound its way to the lighthouse. I couldn't even see Evan's house much through the pine trees near the edge of my property.

I was also suddenly aware that I was alone with a man, albeit hot, that I didn't know. No one would hear me scream.

Taking a step backward into the shelter of the house, I tried again. "There aren't any young girls or teenagers that live up here?"

"Not that I know of. Why?"

"I just... I thought I saw someone walking around outside," I answered vaguely, waving my hand distractedly.

"Nope. Just you and me as far as I know," Evan stuck his hands in his pockets and shrugged. He looked at me for a moment, then down the road toward the lighthouse.

"I'm sorry, I'm not usually this distracted," I commented, my awkwardness pouring out of me. I folded my arms over my chest to hide the fact that I wasn't wearing a bra, but I'm pretty sure he had already noticed that.

"It's all good," Evan smiled with a shrug. "I shoulda called or maybe waited until later to stop by but I didn't have your number obviously and I have to work later so..."

"You work in town?" I asked stupidly, trying desperately not to be awkward but also to keep him around until I felt calmer to be alone. I couldn't possibly tell him about seeing the girl on the back porch suddenly vanish. He'd think I was batshit crazy for sure.

"Yeah, I'm one-third of the Kellner police force," he grinned. "It's a pretty happening place so we have to have three cops on staff just to deal with all the shenanigans."

"Wow... three whole cops," I laughed, "I guess it's better than two and a third." My dark joke escaped my lips before I could stop it and I instantly wished it back.

Evan threw his head back in a laugh. "You're right about that."

I just shrugged and smiled, "Sorry. I'm broken inside and sometimes the darkness sneaks out."

"Who knew I'd be living next door to Wednesday Addams?" Evan snorted. When I rolled my eyes at him, he grinned.

"Hey, serious question though," I thought suddenly, remembering the gnawing from last night. "Do you know of a good exterminator in town? I think I might have a rat problem."

"Rats?" Evan furrowed his brow. "You could talk to Clint Estepp over at the hardware store. He used to do that type of thing. Did you see the rats? Or just their droppings?"

"I've only found mouse droppings but last night I could hear something chewing. It seemed loud and persistent so I'm guessing it was a rat. Maybe a squirrel? Whatever it is, it needs to go."

"That doesn't sound good, especially if it starts chewing on wires and stuff," Evan agreed. He pulled out his phone, "Here, let me give you Clint's number. He's super old school and refuses to have a store website or cell phone."

I took out my phone as he quickly air-dropped Clint's contact to me. I went to put my phone away when my phone chimed again. Glancing at the screen, I realized Evan had sent me a second contact: his own.

"In case you need anything out here," he said quickly, seeming to notice the expression on my face. I wasn't creeped out by it. Maybe I should've been, but I wasn't. I was creeped out by the strange girl I saw on my porch.

"Thanks," I offered with a smile, hoping to portray confidence and stop thinking about the porch. "It makes me feel a little less lonely in this town to have met someone." I texted him my number and watched as he saved it in his phone as Wednesday Addams. A quiet snort escaped me as I shook my head in amusement.

Head still down, he glanced up at me with a sexy, wicked grin on his face. I felt my pulse quicken and not for the first time I wished I'd brushed my hair and gotten dressed. Now that I knew my next-door neighbor was hot I'd have to make my personal hygiene routine more of a priority.

"Well, Hailey, it's been a pleasure," Evan smirked as he slid his phone back into the pocket of his jeans. "I have a few things to do before I get ready for work, but if you need anything, just call or text. I'm right through the trees." He thumbed over his shoulder toward the only other house within a quarter mile.

"Thanks, Evan," I nodded, suddenly a little sad to be alone again. "And thanks for Clint's number. I'll give him a call."

With a wave over his shoulder, Evan was gone, walking back down the road toward his house. I watched him through the window until he disappeared beyond the trees and then sighed, deciding it was time to get back to work.

***

I fell into bed that night exhausted and achy. Muscles I didn't even know I had seemed to be complaining from all of the cleaning I'd done the past two days. As I lay there in my sleeping bag on the lumpy mattress, waiting for sleep to come, my mind thought back over the day and what I needed to accomplish tomorrow.

Clint had told me that I probably just had a mouse problem but that he'd come by and check it out tomorrow afternoon. He was too busy 'mansplaining' about how mice and rats are different and most of the time when people think they have rats or something, it's usually mice. After two minutes of his ramblings, I'd tuned him out, only perking up when he'd said he'd send someone out to survey the issue.

I'd finished all of the cleaning for the most part and brought all of the boxes and bags in from my car. They now sat in a pile right inside the front door. My job for tomorrow, once Clint was done de-mousing my home, was to finish unpacking my meager belongings and then head to town to hit up the grocery store and get a new mattress. If I had to eat one more PB&J sandwich or smell that musty mattress one more night I think I'd scream.

I had just dozed off when something woke me. At first, I couldn't say what it was, but when I went to roll over, I realized that there was pressure on my legs.

Something was lying on them. Something was holding me down.

If I had already gotten my fat ginger cat, I wouldn't have freaked out, but as I was still living alone, my anxiety shot through the roof. I instantly began kicking at the blankets in the darkness, trying to extract myself from the bed as quickly as possible.

The room was murky and dark, the only light source a sliver of moon peering through the window. As I struggled to get out of bed, I reached for the bedside table lamp, but in my haste, I felt it fall to the floor with a shattering sound.

Finally free of the bed, I took large steps to make it to the bedroom door to flip the overhead light on, praying I didn't step on shards of glass in the process. I couldn't hear anything in the room with me over the din of my pounding heart; no growling, no gnawing, no hissing.

Flipping on the light, I whirled around to see what had just been pressing down my legs, holding me to my bed.

There was nothing there.

As my pulse began to slow, my mind continued to race. I had felt something. Just like last night when I heard gnawing. I wasn't crazy, I wasn't making stuff up.

Was I?

I began to shake, anxiety coursing through my body. What was happening to me? Was I losing my mind? At first, I was hearing things, then I was seeing girls on the porch. Now I was feeling like someone was holding me down in my bed.

A laugh escaped my lips. This couldn't be happening, it was too much. Shaking off the absurdity of it, I decided to get the broom and dustpan, before adding 'lamp' to my list of things to buy.

When I stepped back into the bedroom to sweep up the remains of the lamp, I stopped dead in my tracks. There, quite visible around each of my bare ankles, were red lines. Apprehensive, I stooped down to inspect them as they hadn't been there when I went to bed.

It was then that the horrifying truth came flooding into my brain.

They were finger marks.

Fresh, distinct finger marks bruised into my flesh, as though someone had forcefully held me down.

Panic filled me as I felt a scream build in my chest. Was there someone in the house with me? Was the girl from the porch back? If so, where was she now?

Shaking, I dropped the broom at my feet, slowly backed out of my room, and made my way to the kitchen. Sliding a drawer open, I quickly selected the largest knife I owned.

I had to check the rest of the house. I had to prove to myself that I was alone, once and for all. My brain tried to explain away the bruises on my ankles and so far it was failing. My sanity was quickly declining and I needed to obtain some answers if I were to find self-redemption.

Flashlight in one hand, knife in the other, I quickly but thoroughly performed a search of my small cottage home. It appeared I was alone, but if that were true, then how did I get the bruises? How was I awakened by the pressure on my legs?

It was then that I saw the basement door.

It was the last area of the house that I hadn't checked yet. Just thinking about going down there made my skin crawl. Going down there at night was ten times worse.

With a faltering sigh of resignation, I slowly unlatched the door and turned the knob. The hinges groaned quietly as the door swung open to reveal an uneven wooden staircase descending into the darkness. The musty, earthy smell of the basement wafted up and instantly assaulted my nostrils, causing me to sneeze.

I flipped the light switch and groaned inwardly as the low-wattage bulb flared to life, barely illuminating the dismal stairwell.

"Great," I muttered to myself as I slowly descended into murky darkness. Trying to ignore the cobwebs hanging low overhead, I focused on the beam of my flashlight aimed ahead of me.

The old wooden stairs creaked under my weight and I envisioned them breaking, trapping me in the basement for days until Evan happened to come by again.

I shook my head at the thought, trying to turn my over-active imagination off. Steeling my spine, I took the last two steps and found myself standing on the hard-packed dirt floor of the basement.

The light from the stairwell barely penetrated the shadows of the subterranean room. I cast my flashlight beam around the small space and felt a shiver travel down my spine. Overhead, multiple spiderwebs hung from the rafters, their inhabitants watching me from their silken homes.

The basement was merely a dug-out pit under the front half of the cottage, just big enough to house the furnace and hot water tank. Maybe a few plastic totes if you needed storage. The area under the back of the house was more of a low crawl space, barely tall enough for a grown adult to shimmy through on their stomach. The cobwebs covering the hole to enter that section of the basement were intact, telling me that no one had passed through that way in a long time. I turned in a circle, making a quick visual inspection with my flashlight, and determined that other than the spiders, I was alone in the house.

Relieved, though still confused about the bruises on my ankles, I swiftly made my way back to the bottom of the basement stairs. I was halfway up them when suddenly I heard something fall onto the floor somewhere over my head. It sounded like it came from my bedroom.

Now what? I thought to myself as I ran up the last three steps, knife in hand, to determine the source of the sound. Passing through the kitchen on the way to my bedroom I saw nothing amiss. It was as I approached my bedroom door that I heard it. The gnawing sounds from the night before. Clamping my hands over my ears to shut out the auditory assault, I took a deep breath before bursting into my room.

My cell phone lay in the middle of the floor, the charging cord twisted and tangled next to it. I specifically remembered leaving it charging on the kitchen counter.

The hair on the back of my next stood on end and my pulse raced, even as the grinding and gnawing of teeth surrounded me. How had my phone made it into my bedroom? And what was making that wretched sound? I had to find its source or I'd go mad.

The gnawing sound seemed to grow in intensity as I slowly made my way around the room, trying to discern where it was coming from. There! It sounded as though I was right upon it, but there was nothing there except the wall, covered in a hideous flowered wallpaper.

I knelt, feeling over the wooden planks in the floorboards, for what I didn't know. A loose board? A hidden compartment where a rodent had made a nest? I felt nothing amiss, just some random dust bunnies and a dead fly. Frustrated, I began to stand up when the sound came again: a gnawing and clacking of teeth. It was the eeriest thing and if I didn't find the source soon, I feared I'd go crazy.

That's when it hit me. The sound was coming from inside the wall.

Still standing on my knees, I began to feel around the wall, looking for any anomalies or weak spots. The floral wallpaper, aged and peeling in places, seemed to mock my efforts. Knowing I was going to be painting the room soon anyway, I quickly decided now was as good of a time as any to get started on removing the wallpaper.

Finding a furled edge, I slid my finger underneath and began pulling it away from the old drywall. The wallpaper came away easy enough, the glue long ago losing its effectiveness. As I continued pulling off chunks of paper and discarding it at my feet, I strained to listen for the gnawing sound.

At the moment, it was quiet. It had to be some animal in the wall, listening intently as I got closer and closer to its hiding place.

Soon, I found myself up against the old chest of drawers, and keen on checking behind it, I began pulling it away from the wall. It was much heavier than I'd anticipated but after a few moments of pushing and pulling (and some profanity), I was finally able to get behind it to survey the wall.

It was then that the gnawing sound began again, almost turning into a loud hum. Part of me wanted to cover my ears from the auditory assault and run away, but the other part of me suddenly felt like I was onto something. Something big.

Through the humming sound, I was able to focus on the task at hand, and that was when I noticed an imperfection in the drywall, down near the baseboard. Up until that point, that section of wall had been hidden from view by the antique dresser.

Squatting down once again, I leaned forward and gently pressed a hand on the imperfection. It was a soft spot under the wallpaper, the area giving under the light pressure of my hand. What was back there?

I grasped the edges of the wallpaper and began pulling it back as quickly as I could without tearing it too much. Slowly, carefully, the drywall was revealed, and that is when I saw it. A small hole, roughly five inches wide and six inches tall, had been crudely knocked into the wall some ten inches from the floor. Who would do such a thing and why?

The hole was dark and when I tried to look inside, I was afraid to get too close at first. I'd seen too many horror movies where something hideous and undead would jump out of such a hole and I was not interested in that.

But, at last, curiosity got the better of me.

I grabbed my flashlight from where I'd left it on the counter in the kitchen and then headed back to the hole I'd just uncovered. That's when I realized that the toothy clicking sounds had stopped. Relieved, and somewhat apprehensive, I decided to finish this once and for all. I was tired of all the animal activity around this place and the faster I got to the bottom of it, the better.

Shining the flashlight into the murky depths of the hole in the wall, I could see nothing except cobwebs and dust. But there had to be a reason for the hole, right? Maybe there was something in the wall, the mere thought causing me to shiver. I didn't want to put my hand down in a creepy dark hole that may or may not have an animal living in it.

But it had to be done. I needed answers and I needed them now.

Sighing deeply to collect my thoughts, I ignored my racing heart. Rubbing my sweaty palms on my fleece-clad thighs, I decided to make my move. Slowly, carefully, I stuck my hand into the aperture in the wall, cautiously feeling around. I tried to turn my brain off and not think of what kind of creepy crawly made that hole it's home.

Something skittered across my hand and I withdrew it with a squeal. A shiver ran down my spine as I tried to calm myself. My hand was covered in dust and cobwebs, but thankfully no spiders.

Once my pulse was back to a normal level, I slid my hand into the hole a second time. At first, I felt nothing but dust and dead space, and then suddenly, my fingertip touched something cold and smooth. Curiosity and excitement coursed through me as I reached further into the hole. When I bumped the item again, I wrapped my fingers around it and carefully pulled it upward. As I extracted it from its hiding place I realized it was an old glass jar with a rusted lid. Inside were some kind of red and white beads. I gently rolled the dusty jar around in my hand, trying to get a better look at the beads when I let out a scream.

They weren't beads. They were human teeth.

Another scream tore from my throat as I dropped the jar on the floor near my feet and watched in horror as it rolled under the antique dresser, its gruesome contents making a tinkling sound.

I hopped up from my seated position on the floor, eager to bolt, when the gnawing sound began again, this time louder than it had ever been. Covering my ears from the onslaught, I let out another scream and ran from the room and out of the house.

The night air felt cool on my heated skin as I ran barefoot through the woods. I was going mad! This couldn't be happening. First the creepy girl on my porch, then something pressing me into my mattress, the hideous gnawing sound, and now this! A little jar of teeth!

I tripped then, snagging my toe on a tree root. Landing on the soft, pine needle-laden ground with a grunt, I cast a glance behind me at my house. My new house that was supposed to be my forever home. Now I couldn't wait to be done with it!

My heart was racing as I tried to catch my breath, and yet I continued to sob. I couldn't even hear the sound of the waves crashing on the rocks below over the sound of my anguish.

I was about to turn around and stand up when movement caught my eye. In the living room window of my house was the silhouette of someone watching me. Another chill ran down my spine as I stood up and bounded through the woods to Evan's house. His patrol car was in the driveway and his living room light was still on, a beacon in a time of torment.

I quickly made it across the yard and up the gravel driveway. Climbing the porch stairs and pounding on the door,

I took in great gulps of air, trying to calm myself. Tears and snot coursed down my face as I shook uncontrollably.

He answered the door, a look of grave concern etched into his handsome face. "Hailey? What's wrong? Are you okay?" He stepped back and gently ushered me into his home, but not before I saw him glance over my shoulder, surveying the woods beyond. He must have just gotten home from work as I was vaguely aware that he was still wearing his police uniform.

Once I was seated on his couch, covered in a soft fleece blanket, I told Evan everything. About the creepy girl on the porch, the feeling of being held down in my bed, the nightly wake-up calls of gnawing and chewing sounds. I don't think he believed most of what I said, even though he remained patient and quiet until I mentioned the hole in the wall. It was when I told him about the little jar of teeth and showed him my ankles that Evan became very interested, asking all sorts of questions.

After some persuasion, he finally talked me into showing him the jar. I didn't want to go back home. I didn't want to hear the chewing sounds, see the ghostly apparitions, or touch the macabre glass container of human dentition.

With some reluctance, I slowly climbed into his patrol car and we drove back to my house in silence. I was still shaking from fear, anxiety... perhaps both, and every fiber in me wanted to bolt but I was still barefoot, wearing fleece pajama pants and an old Beatles tee shirt.

The front door was still ajar from where I'd fled earlier. Evan took the lead, a figure of confidence in his uniform, while I followed timidly behind waiting for the gnawing sounds to start up again. I didn't want to go back into the house, much less the bedroom.

"Do I have to go in?" I asked, slowing my pace as I watched him climb my front steps. He cast a glance over his shoulder.

"I suppose not, but then you'd be out here all by yourself," he shrugged. I sucked in a quick breath and quickly followed him inside.

"Why are you so excited about a little jar of teeth?" I asked, still horrified that he wanted to see it. Who in their right mind would want to see it? I had just settled on the fact that it was probably only because he was in law enforcement and it was something he should look into when his next words made my blood run cold.

"Because it... it could be the key to solving a cold case," he sighed, running his fingers through his dark hair. "A serial killer cold case," he casually added as we entered my bedroom and he looked around at the mess I'd made.

"What?" My eyes went round with the horror of it all. I watched Evan's expression as he seemed to wrestle within himself over how much he should tell me. Eventually, with a sigh of resignation, he reached over and took my hand. He was silent for a moment, quietly comforting me with his closeness. Finally, he spoke.

"They called him 'The Dentist' on account he would pull the girls' teeth out, one by one, while they were still alive."

"How do you know that?"

"Because there was one girl who survived just long enough. She came into the station in rough shape. Most of her teeth were already gone. She'd been so distraught that she'd been unable to even speak to us or answer our questions. We weren't able to get much from her except the word 'more', which she'd written on a napkin right before having some kind of epileptic episode. She never regained consciousness but it was then that we knew that there were other girls. Other victims."

"How many?" I asked, afraid to ask but needing to know, just the same.

"She was the first girl that made contact with the police. They thought she'd been taken by someone who knew her, or just a one-and-done type of guy. But a week or so after she passed away, someone found another girl, this time washed up dead on the shore just east of here. Every last tooth had been pulled from her skull."

I felt myself shiver involuntarily, the sheer terror of what that girl must have gone through playing through my mind. Bile rose in my throat and I tried desperately to keep it down. I focused on Evan as he bent low to inspect the little jar of teeth I'd sent rolling halfway under the dresser. He slid on a latex glove from his pocket and carefully picked it up before continuing his tale.

"In the end, they found four bodies, each missing all of their teeth. All the girls were local teenagers. Two other girls disappeared around that time as well, but their bodies were never found. One was said to have been seen down South somewhere but... I don't know. People talk and come to their own conclusions. Over the years, the two that never turned up were just chalked up to being runaways." He shrugged then, a look of frustration marring his handsome face. Holding up the little jar of teeth to the light, he rotated it around to inspect. The small bloodied teeth shifted slightly at the movement like some kind of macabre snowglobe.

We walked into the kitchen and sat at the table, each eyeing the glass jar in his hand apprehensively. "I'll take these down to the station, and get them sent out to the forensic lab to confirm, but really? Where else could a bunch of teeth come from?" He turned to me then, setting the jar on the table between us. "If this is those girls' teeth, then you just ripped this case wide open."

"Go me," I used sarcasm to hide my apprehension. Had I bought a murder house? Were innocent girls killed here, their teeth yanked out of their skulls for the sheer enjoyment of some madman? I sat picking at a scratch on the old oak table, trying to keep my shaking hands busy.

Evan reached over and laid a hand on mine. "Hailey, look at me." I slowly slid my gaze up his chest to his face, stopping when I found his blue eyes watching me with concern.

"Hailey, this isn't your fault," he comforted, "This could have happened to anyone. This case has plagued the town of Kellner for years and finally, it seems we might finally have an answer."

***

The next two days were the longest of my life. I kept jumping every time I got a call or a text, hoping it was news about the little jar of teeth. I knew the DNA test results would take time to come back from the lab, but I was hoping for some kind of information. I was exhausted from lack of sleep due to the confounded gnawing and chewing sounds, and now strange whispers, but luckily for me, there had been no further assaults on my person. My bruises were starting to heal, taking on various shades of the rainbow.

I avoided the house for the afternoon by taking myself on a picnic in the backyard, overlooking the sea. I had spread an old quilt near the cliffside and, book and lunch in hand, I made every effort to mentally escape the nightmare my life had become.

I had just finished my apple and was enjoying the warmth of the sun on my skin, the sea breeze mussing my hair, when my cell phone rang. Glancing at the screen, my pulse raced. It was Evan.

"Hello?" I answered, willing a smile into my voice. I failed.

"Hi, Hailey, it's Evan. I'm just calling to let you know that we have an update on the little jar of teeth you found." He sounded tired, maybe even apprehensive.

"And...?" I pressed gently, needing to hear the truth before I screamed.

"The thing is, Hailey, there were only four known victims..." Evan stated.

"And...?" I repeated, this time slightly more agitated, willing him to get to the point.

"And well, when the lab analyzed and counted the teeth in the jar... there were enough for six victims."

"Meaning what exactly?"

"Meaning your house has just become a possible crime scene and they are writing up a warrant as I speak."

"What?" I asked incredulously, trying to process his words. Six victims? More bodies? My house was a possible crime scene? I felt the world around me begin to spin and suddenly felt light-headed and ill.

"Do they think the bodies are here? *Inside my house*?" I asked weakly, the ghostly apparitions I'd been seeing at night suddenly making sense. Never usually one to believe in such nonsense, I'd become a believer the past week. The creepy girls watching me, whispering to me... even the gnawing sounds in the wall all suddenly made sense.

They had to be in the house.

They were just waiting to be found. Grinding teeth they didn't have, walking around a house that wasn't theirs. Trapped in space between life and death. They'd been brought to this house, bound and kept as little pets, and then tortured and killed. And yet they had unfinished business.

Something was holding them here and I meant to help them. They just wanted to be found. They wanted to go home.

"Tear the house up," I said, turning away from the cottage to face the sea. "I don't even care what you need to do to it. Just find them."

***

Within a few hours, all three of Kellner's police force, along with the state crime scene investigation unit, were setting up on my front lawn. Black and yellow crime scene tape had already been placed as a barrier to keep the growing media and onlookers back. My anxiety was all over the place. Never had I wished to be anywhere but my own home so bad. With the arrival of the cadaver dog team, my stomach lurched and I was forced to run for the bathroom.

The dogs were here for one reason only: to look for human remains.

After emptying my stomach of my meager breakfast and anxiety-induced bile, I stood staring at myself in the mirror as I rinsed my mouth. My face was pale and sweaty. Dark circles, from stress and lack of sleep, had taken up residence under my eyes. In short, I looked like a shell of my former self, and I'd only lived in that house for a week. How much longer would I have survived if I hadn't found the little jar of teeth? Would the girls have continued to haunt me at night? Would I have heard the gnawing sounds within the walls until I'd gone mad?

Suddenly, there was a knock at the bathroom door, jarring me from my thoughts.

"Hailey? Are you okay there?" Evan's voice sounded muffled. I reached over and turned the knob, opening the door a crack. He gave me a small smile, his blue eyes scanning over me as though looking for signs I was falling apart.

"Freaking out a little. I'll be okay once all of this is over," I sighed, opening the door the rest of the way. Evan reached out and I stepped into his arms, his uniform and vest making him feel bulky. His radio, clipped to his shoulder, crackled to life next to my ear, but we ignored it.

"I'm sorry this is happening to you," he mumbled into my hair, "but I do hope they find something today. Those girls need to be returned to their families." I nodded my agreement when Chief Louman stepped into view.

"We're ready to get started," the older officer announced with a nod to Evan and me. We pulled away from each other and quickly made our way outside. Evan led me over toward the perimeter to wait out of the view of onlookers and media and for that, I was grateful.

I don't know how long I sat there, quietly watching law enforcement search my home and property. I hoped they'd find nothing, but in my heart, I knew they would.

It came as no surprise a few hours later that the atmosphere shifted. I'd been dozing in the passenger seat of Evan's cruiser, listening to the waves crash against the rocks far below while the gulls cried overhead when suddenly excited voices could be heard coming from the house.

Sitting up abruptly, I watched out the window of the police cruiser as two officers from the state came out of my front door, deep in conversation, gesticulating wildly. Opening the car door, I quickly climbed out and headed toward the porch in search of Evan.

"Ma'am, you can't go in there. This is a crime scene," one of the officers informed me, holding his palm up to halt me.

"This is my house. I'm the one that found the teeth," I informed them, trying to stand on my toes to see past them. Evan was inside somewhere. Surely he could vouch for my presence.

"Ma'am, I understand that, but you can't—"

I didn't wait for him to finish. Slipping around him, I was through the front door before he or his partner could stop me.

Voices could be heard, speaking in hushed tones, from somewhere in the vicinity of my bedroom. I quickly headed in that direction, fully expecting to feel the strong grip of the state police who'd told me to stay out pressing down on my shoulder.

Everything happened so fast as I stumbled into the bedroom, narrowly avoiding the officer's meaty palm as he came up behind me. Evan, squatting next to a crime scene technician, looked up as I barged into the room.

"Sorry, boys," the officer from the porch smirked, rolling his eyes in my direction. "I told her she couldn't come in here..." He reached for me again but I dodged away, stepping closer to Evan.

"And I told you, Officer, that this is my house and I found the damn teeth," I snapped. "I've been nothing but helpful during all of this and if it wasn't for me, you'd still have unsolved murders hanging over this town."

The officer glowered at me with disdain, a look echoed by his coworker. Evan, however, seemed to sense that I was near the end of my rope.

"Hey, Sudansky, it's all good," he smiled at the other officer. "She can stay here, as long as she doesn't touch anything." The last part of his statement was directed toward me, his way of telling me to stay cool.

Sudansky, the officer from the porch, didn't seem too pleased but finally relented. After he and his partner headed back outside, I turned to see what Evan and the CSI had been up to.

My bedroom had been pulled apart, the furniture re-arranged. But the most disturbing thing I could see was the tool marks on the wide wooden floor planks where my bed had been. There were deep gouges in the planks, possibly made by someone prying the boards up.

"Are they under my floor?" I asked in a nervous whisper. "Have I been sleeping over them this whole time?" I felt my pulse start to race at the thought of dead girls being hidden in the floor under my bed.

"The dogs alerted here," Evan explained grimly. "When we moved the bed frame, we found the tool marks."

The CSI on the floor looked up at Evan and waited for his nod to go ahead before slipping a crowbar in between the floorboards. I watched silently, both terrified and excited about what we may find.

The nails made a loud squealing sound as they released their hold on the wide planks. Evan and I held our breath in anticipation of what we'd find inside. Finally, after some tugging and manipulation, the CSI pulled the board free to reveal the murky area below.

There, illuminated in the flashlight beam, lay a mummified human skeleton, its gaping mouth devoid of teeth. The remaining bits of flesh and hair that clung to the skull made my stomach roil. Surprisingly, the smell hadn't been noticeable until the floorboard had been removed and the long-stagnant air stirred up.

I rocked back on my feet, suddenly feeling lightheaded. Dear God, who was that girl under my bed? And who had done that to her?

My mind flashed back to the creepy apparition on the screened-in porch on my first day here. Had she been trying to get my attention, trying to help me find her so that she could go home once and for all?

And then it hit me. Didn't Evan say there were enough teeth in the little jar for six victims? The girl in the floor only made five. Where was the sixth girl?

"Is this the only place the dog's told you about?" I asked, my mind reeling and wondering where number six could be.

"Yes, unfortunately," Evan said grimly. "It'll be a while before we are done processing the scene. You may want to get a hotel room for the night. We should be out of here by tomorrow."

I nodded numbly. This whole situation was insane and my brain was having a difficult time processing. A dead girl had been entombed in the floor directly under where I'd been sleeping since moving to Kellner.

"I'd like to get some clothes and personal items if I can," I mumbled as tears pooled in my eyes. The dark hole in the floor pulled my gaze but I resisted. I didn't want to see the grotesque scene any further.

"Sure, just don't touch anything over there," Evan thumbed over his shoulder toward the gruesome scene.

Quickly opening the drawers in my dresser, I grabbed a few clothing items, including my favorite hoodie for comfort. Shoving them into my backpack, I nearly ran from the room to collect my items from the bathroom.

***

Within moments, I was headed towards Kellner, away from the house of horrors and gnashing teeth. My choices were extremely slim for the night as Kellner only had one motel; a twelve-room, single-story brick building with a flickering neon sign that boasted "Free Wifi" and a Continental breakfast.

I pulled into the nearly empty parking lot as the sun dipped low in the sky. Quickly making my way into the motel's office to check in, I suddenly realized how hungry I was. I hadn't eaten all day as I was too stressed over the search at my house.

The office door slammed shut behind me, tinkling a bell overhead. The front desk was deserted.

"Hello?" I called, straining my ears for signs of another person. In the background, a small flat-screened TV played the nightly news at a low volume. "Hello? Is anyone here?" I called again.

"Ahh! Sorry about that!" came a woman's voice from down a hallway to the left of the desk. "I'm coming!"

A second later, a tall, curvy woman with teased-out bleached blond hair waltzed up to the desk. Her makeup was bright and almost garish, matching her outfit. Her plastic nametag said her name was Becky.

"I just had to run to the little girl's room," she smiled, her face splitting into a bright, welcoming smile. "You need a room, honey?"

"Yes, please. One night, maybe two," I smiled back as I slid my credit card across the counter. "Hey, do you recommend any place that delivers food around here?"

"Oh, well Bucky's Pizza is amazing, and Guiseppe's has Italian. The Sock Hop is more hamburgers and fries—kinda has a 50s diner feel, you get me?" Becky threw another mega-watt smile in my direction as she entered something into her computer.

"Awesome, thanks," I grinned, my stomach growling loudly as if on cue. We laughed and then finished getting me checked into room number 12.

"Oh, so you bought the old Boyd place? Out on the point?" Becky asked as she entered my address into the computer.

"Yeah," I mumbled, thinking about the skeleton in my floor.

"I bet there are a lot of updates that need to be done, huh? Old Charlie lived there for years with only his son to take care of him," Becky shook her head in dismay. "He was a sweet old man, always helping out at all of the football games down at the high school. He ran the concession stand, that is until he got too sick to do it anymore."

Too bad she doesn't know that ol' Charlie was a serial killer who ripped girl's teeth from their skulls before killing them, I thought to myself. It wasn't my place to say anything about the skeleton found in my house, or the investigation so I kept my snide comments to myself.

When I said nothing, Becky seemed to pick up on the fact that I didn't want to discuss Charlie, and quickly finished processing my check-in.

"Here you go," she handed me a yellow plastic key fob with a large '12' painted on it. From it dangled a single key. "If you need anything just call the front desk. Ice is right around the corner. Check-out is at 11:00 am." She smiled at me again, but it didn't seem as bright or welcoming as before. Was it because I hadn't seemed excited to learn about Charlie's accolades as a small-town gem?

"Thanks, Becky," I cast her a friendly smile. "And thanks for the dinner recommendations."

When I only received a nod from her, I quickly shoved my credit card into my purse and, key in hand, went to find my room.

Room 12 looked like any other roadside motel: ugly geometric-patterned bedspread hiding God only knew what kind of stains, cheap, mass-produced artwork on the walls, an array of brochures for local treasures (Kellner apparently only had two), and a faux leather-bound Bible shoved in the drawer next to the bed.

I decided on pizza and after calling Bucky's to order a small sausage and pepperoni pie, I had just enough time for a quick shower before it would arrive.

While I ate my pizza, I decided to do some internet sleuthing. I typed in Charlie Boyd's name, along with 'Kellner' to see what I could find out about the previous owner of my house and possibly the little jar of teeth.

I began wondering why I hadn't heard his name before. Why hadn't it been on my mortgage paperwork? The seller's name had been some property management company. None of it made any sense.

According to my online search, Charleston Leeman Boyd, age 94, died on April 23rd of this year after a long illness. He'd been an active volunteer with youth activities at the high school for nearly forty years.

"I bet you were, you monster," I muttered to myself before taking another bite of pizza.

His obituary claimed he was ex-military, had worked for the city for over five decades, and was survived by his son, Andrew Fletcher Boyd of Topeka, daughter Abigail Diane Powalski (nee Boyd) of San Francisco, four grandchildren, and six great-grandchildren. His wife and siblings had all preceded him in death.

I decided to take notes. It seemed that ol' Charlie didn't have much family, but maybe they could offer more information about—

About what?

This was a matter for the police. It wasn't up to me to play Sherlock Holmes and try to track a serial killer's movements, right?

With a frustrated sigh, I tossed my phone down and laid back. Staring at the ceiling, thoughts began swirling through my brain and before long, I fell into a fitful sleep.

Girls with bloodied faces, their toothless mouths open wide, crept through my thoughts. The gnawing sound began buzzing in my ears, chewing and grinding. The girls turned their hideous faces toward me, reaching out for me with bruised and blooding arms. Their moans and distorted whispers assaulted my ears, along with the grinding of bone on bone. Teeth.

I woke with a start, sucking in large gulps of air. My body was sweaty, and my hair clung to my neck. I lay atop the ugly bedspread, willing my heart rate to slow, and began to shake.

When would the nightmares end? I couldn't go on like this. They'd found one of the victims, so why weren't the nightmares stopping? Would I be haunted by the girls for the rest of my life?

Shakily, I got off the bed, the pizza box still lying where I'd left it, and headed toward the bathroom. I wanted another shower. I needed to wash away the fear, sweat, and anxiety that seemed to have me in its clutches.

After standing in the shower, water coursing over me and carrying my anxiety away with it down the drain, I turned the tap off and reached for a towel. Pulling back the shower curtain, I wrapped the towel around myself and carefully stepped out.

Steam swirled in the small room despite the weak-sounding exhaust fan above. I quickly dried off, turned toward the sink to brush my teeth, and nearly screamed.

In the condensation on the mirror was a message: the letters F, L, and E. To my horror, I watched as more letters slowly began forming on the steamed-up glass. A 'T' and a 'C' were slowly joined by others. Before long, a word appeared.

"Fletcher," I read in a shaking voice. As I reached out toward the mirror, I saw movement behind me and let out a scream. It was the girl from my porch. The dead girl with the toothless maw. We locked eyes in the mirror, my breath hitching in my chest.

"Did Fletcher do this to you?" I asked shakily. The apparition in the mirror slowly nodded. Tears welled in my eyes as sorrow filled my heart.

"Did Charlie Boyd have anything to do with it?"

Again the girl nodded even as she began to fade from view. Frantic, I whirled around, looking for her. I still had so many unanswered questions, but it was too late. She was gone.

With shaking legs, I made my way out of the bathroom, a sob building in my chest. Had Charlie and Fletcher worked together to hunt girls, torture them by pulling all of their teeth out, and who knows what else, only to kill them and cast their remains aside?

It was too much. I couldn't process it. I wished I had never come to this God-forsaken town. Kellner wasn't the Mayberry it claimed to be.

I had to find out who Fletcher was and where he lived. I needed some kind of proof before I went to the police or they'd laugh me out of the station. Who would believe that I'd gotten the information from a dead girl? Even the thought of it sounded ridiculous.

After quickly throwing on some clothes, I grabbed my phone again and resumed my Google search, this time for Fletcher and Kellner. I added 'Boyd' almost as an after-thought. Within seconds, the search results appeared on screen, and to my horror, I finally had some answers. With a gasp of revulsion, I threw my phone back on the bed as though it were a snake.

***

"Ahh, Miss Sullivan, back so soon?" the realtor greeted me as I stepped into his office. He smiled then, his face splitting to reveal his crooked coffee-stained teeth.

"Yes, Mr. Boyd. I'll need your services again," I stated, getting directly to the point. "I want to sell my house."

"But you've only just moved in!" he exclaimed with a robust laugh. "You haven't even given Kellner a chance! Why do you want to sell so soon?"

"Well, it's a small town and so I'm sure you've heard by now," I began, watching his reaction. If my hunch was correct, he could get into legal trouble. He'd sold me property without disclosing the home's macabre past. He knew about the cold case. He knew about The Dentist.

"Oh... yes, I did hear about that," he muttered, digging through the papers on his desk before finding a pair of reading glasses. Wiping the lenses with the hem of his green shirt, he watched me. "It is unfortunate that that girl was buried up there all those years. Did they find the other one?"

My pulse began to pound in my chest and my breathing increased though I tried to hide it before he noticed.

"The other one?" I asked coyly. It was better to play dumb than give away too much. How did he know about the sixth victim? Evan had told me that only he and his chief knew that fact so how did Mr. Boyd know unless my assumption was correct?

"They said there were at least six victim's teeth in that little jar of teeth you found," Mr. Boyd supplied, raising an eyebrow at me. I said nothing at first, mostly from the shock that he even knew about the jar of teeth being found, much less the number of teeth inside. Small-town whispers. Damnit!

I sat there in silence, my mind racing to form questions that would provide the answers I needed but also get me out of there alive.

"Your first name isn't Andrew like your father is it?" I asked, watching Mr. Boyd for any tells. His face reddened and a vein in his forehead stood out. I was making him sweat. "Your real name is Fletcher Andrew Boyd, just a flip-flop of your father's name, am I right?"

"What makes you say that?" he emitted a bark of a laugh that held no humor.

"Oh, just a quick internet search, a phone call to your dad asking to speak to Fletcher... He gave me Fletcher's phone number when I told him I was an old friend from high school. When I ran a number search, well, it matched up with Boyd Realty in Kellner. That's when I found out that your legal name is Fletcher Andrew Boyd but you go by Andrew now, just like Pops." I grinned at him, knowing I was right when he broke out in a sweat.

"Where's the other girl, Fletch?" I asked, hoping my cell phone was picking up all of this. It was hidden in the front pocket of my hoodie.

"What else do you think you know?" he snapped, glaring at me over his reading glasses.

I didn't know anything else, but I wasn't about to tell him that, so I just grinned at him, feigning confidence. Inside, my body was churning with liquid anxiety and I was trying not to visibly shake.

"Don't play dumb with me," he snapped, his entire countenance suddenly shifting. "So what? My legal name is Fletcher. Who the hell cares?" he glowered at me, his crooked coffee-stained teeth visible in his sneer.

"I do. Especially when you didn't disclose that you sold me a murder house."

"Who do you think sold you that house? Me? The paperwork said something to the effect of Fire Storm Property Management," Mr. Boyd stated, trying to sound surprised but failing epically.

"Ah, I'm glad you brought that up. According to public records, Fire Storm Property Management is owned by one Fletcher A. Boyd from Kellner. You knew damn well what was hidden in that house," I snapped with righteous indignation.

Mr. Boyd stared at me with hate in his eyes for a moment, anger seeping out of him with every breath.

"That was my grandpa's house," he finally admitted with a sigh. He leaned forward over his desk, head hung in dismay. After a moment, he looked back up at me, a sad look on his face.

"Come with me," he stood and stepped around his desk. "I want to show you something. Something that I think will help you with with all of this. I probably should have given it to the police long ago, but I... I didn't want to ruin my grandpa's last days on Earth."

"You didn't want him to suffer like his victims?" I asked, sarcasm filling my voice as I reluctantly got up to follow him. Maybe the dead girl meant Fletcher had the key to solving the crime? Not that he'd killed the girls?

I followed Mr. Boyd down a short hallway that was dead-ended with a closed door. He opened it to reveal a flight of stairs descending into the darkness. Reaching up he pulled the string, illuminating the stairwell.

"I use this old basement for storage. Grandpa gave me some boxes of stuff to keep here. That's how I found out things about him. Dark things," Mr. Boyd stated gravely. He stepped to the side and gestured for me to go first.

Without thinking, I stepped around him to descend the stairs and that is when I realized my mistake. I suddenly felt myself being shoved forward and my body falling end over end down the flight of stairs. My head hit various treads on the way down, along with my hips and arms.

By the time I made it to the bottom of the stairwell, everything had gone black.

***

When I regained consciousness, I couldn't move. I found myself strapped to a wooden chair, my arms in leather restraints at my side. Pain coursed through me as I tried looking around. My right eye was nearly swollen shut and my jaw hurt to move it. Cautiously, I felt around in my mouth with my tongue and sighed in relief. All of my teeth were still accounted for.

It seemed that I was still in Mr. Boyd's basement; the concrete floor, the cinder block walls, the boxes and junk piled everywhere. Everything was silent except for my ragged breathing. Where had Mr. Boyd gone?

I tried to turn my head to look around, pulling at my restraints as I did so. My head pounded and every sound I made seemed to be amplified. Even the sound of the pilot light on the hot water tank was stressful to me.

Suddenly, the basement door opened and Mr. Boyd descended, feigning surprise when he found me lucid.

"Ahh! Miss Sullivan! You're awake," he exclaimed with a broad fake smile that reminded me of a used car salesman who knew he was selling you a lemon.

"Fuck you," I spat at him, pulling at the restraints again. When I tried to move my legs, pain stabbed through my left leg from where I'd fallen. It was then that I also realized that my ankles were strapped to the chair legs. I was completely and utterly immobile. Anger coursed through me, churning with fear and anxiety.

"Now, now... Is that any way to talk to your elders?" Mr. Boyd asked with a sneer.

"You killed those girls didn't you?" I ground out, glaring over at Mr. Boyd despite my eye being swollen shut.

"Depends on which girls you're talking about." A snake-like grin spread across his face.

"The toothless ones," I hissed, "like the one found in my floor yesterday. You and your grandfather killed them."

"Of course. I helped him with *everything*," Mr. Boyd laughed, the sound holding no humor. "He taught me everything he knew about life, love... hunting."

"Too bad you weren't hunting deer," I quipped sarcastically. This caused Mr. Boyd to throw his head back and bellow.

"Very true, very true," he laughed darkly. "It's fun hunting the girls. Watching them squirm and fight when they realize there is no escape. When the screaming starts is when it really gets fun."

"Wait... what do you mean 'it's' fun? As in 'it is' fun? Are there more than six victims?" I asked, suddenly feeling ill all over again. "Are you *still* killing girls and taking their teeth?"

"Grandpa only killed six. The last one of his I dumped over the cliff into the sea. Weighed her down with cinderblocks," he shrugged, unconcerned.

"And you?" I asked, not wanting to know the answer, but asking nonetheless.

Mr. Boyd flashed me his crooked smile once again before stepping behind me. I kept expecting a knife to slit my throat or something to hit me over the head. Instead, I could hear him moving around behind me doing something.

"I always go out of state for my hunts. Makes it harder to track," his voice was muffled as he moved around the room behind me.

Suddenly, he walked back around to stand in front of me and held out his hand. In it was a little jar of teeth, this one much fuller than the one I'd found.

"When I'm done with you, I'll have twenty-two girls." He gave the little jar a shake, causing the teeth to shift inside. The tinkling sound of the teeth in the jar was my final undoing.

I let out a feral scream, willing anyone to hear me, to save me, but it was all for nothing because it was then that I noticed the metal dental extractors in his other hand.

"Open wide, Miss Sullivan," he said with an evil grin.

10

THE ALASKAN TERROR

I returned to consciousness with a start, sitting up and gasping for breath. My head throbbed, pulsing pain with each beat of my heart. Reaching up to touch my forehead to assess the source of the pain, I winced, quickly pulling my fingers back. They were covered in blood, red and sticky. What happened? I felt dazed, confused, and unable to form a coherent thought. Slowly, unsteadily, I rose to my knees and looked around, surveying my surroundings. It was then that the wind shifted, bringing with it the scent of fuel and something burning. And then I remembered. The plane. I turned to see the wreckage, the source of the stench assaulting my nostrils.

The twisted, broken carcass of the Cessna bush plane lay smoldering just thirty feet or so from where I sat. The ground behind it was plowed and furrowed from where the plane had slid on the terrain and came to a screeching halt against a tree before bursting into flames. The flames, at present, were small but the smoke damage was evident on what was left of the cockpit. The yellow and blue tail of the Cessna stuck up at an awkward angle, mostly undamaged. Pieces of the plane lay scattered around the area, bent or scorched.

I stood up carefully, my head still throbbing and my stomach churning. Looking around at my surroundings, I tried to determine where I was exactly. Yes, I knew I was in the Alaskan Bush, but where? As far as I could see, the landscape appeared wild and natural with no signs of human life. Trying not to panic, I took in the mountains, far off in the distance, that were already topped with white—termination dust as the Alaskans called it. Each year, at the end of Autumn, we'd watch the snow line slowly creep down the mountainside, effectively declaring that winter was coming. Luckily for me, there was no snow where I was yet, just craggy tundra, crunching under my feet. From my vantage point, a few pine and birch trees were scattered around among some tall bushes. Sighing, I knew I would have to get to higher ground to see anything else.

I slowly turned and walked through the detritus, making my way to the plane. Maybe I could radio for help? Maybe my cell phone was still in there, unharmed? And where was the pilot? The pilot! I quickly panicked, looking around with greater urgency. I stood on the tips of my toes, straining to look into the fuselage. At first, I could see nothing in the darkened interior except for vague outlines of the remains of rubber storage totes. I didn't see anything that resembled human remains. Where was the pilot?

I had only recently met the pilot, Jerry McClane when I had talked to him at a party. I had grown up in Eagle River, Alaska, and had gone out in various bush planes only twice before when I was a kid. I had always loved the idea of flying, of being free to go wherever I wanted without the confines of roads. To be able to go anywhere on a whim, no matter how remote.

At my friend's house party, I remember overhearing a guy I'd seen around a few times, telling a story of a risky landing he'd had a few months prior. A small group of people had gathered around to listen to the yarn, greatly embellished for our benefit, I'm sure. When the story was over, the crowd commenting and laughing at his antics, Jerry took an elaborate bow and grinned from ear to ear. As the crowd dispersed, I remained to ask him some questions as I had been thinking about getting my pilot's license.

"Hi. You're Jerry, right?" I asked, suddenly feeling a little awkward. Small talk was not a strong suit of mine. Jerry nodded, taking a sip out of his red plastic cup.

"Guilty!" he grinned. "You're Devon's friend, right?"

"Kate," I nodded, shaking his extended hand. "I've been thinking about getting my pilot's license. Your story has me rethinking that though," I said with a laugh.

"Oh! It isn't that bad!" Jerry shrugged. "You should do it! It's the best feeling in the world. I've been flying since I was like twelve. I mean, my dad was there with me of course, but he let me take control and go where I wanted. He would just read or listen to music." He smiled, lost in the memory. "When I was old enough, I started working with other aviators, delivering supplies to different bush villages. That's what I do now. Make deliveries, repair planes, fly around for the fun of it." He paused to take another drink. "You should go up with me sometime. I have a small delivery to make Thursday morning if you want to go. Shouldn't be more than a couple of hours. You in?"

"Sure! I'd love that," I smiled, trying to rein in my excitement. "Thank you!" We exchanged phone numbers and promised to stay in touch, looking forward to Thursday.

***

Now, amid the smoking fuselage, I couldn't believe that party had been less than a week ago. I couldn't believe this had happened. Here I was, a passenger of a wrecked Cessna, stranded alone in the middle of the Alaskan Bush. I had to find Jerry. Swallowing the panic rising in my chest, I made my way to the other side of the plane and that's when I saw him.

Jerry lay in a crumpled heap just yards from the burnt-out aircraft. His clothes looked singed and melted in various areas, and his scalp was a mix of red, bloody flesh, and blackened, singed hair. I ran to his limp form as fast as my aching legs would allow. As I approached him, I knew there was little hope that he had made it through the crash alive. His face, or what was left of it, was a blackened yet bloody mess. His eyes appeared open, lifeless, and unseeing, the eyelids rolled back and nearly obliterated. I barely made it five feet away before vomiting up the contents of my stomach and then dry heaving. My heart rate elevated, and sweat ran down my spine. When my stomach had calmed, I sat down roughly, wiping at the bile taste in my mouth. My body began shaking uncontrollably and my head throbbed. I didn't know what to do. I was alone, in the middle of nowhere, left to my own devices. Tears ran down my cheeks and I sat there blubbering and snotting like an idiot, but I didn't care.

I don't how long I sat there. I looked over at Jerry's body, noticing the smell for the first time. Not that of decay, but of cooked meat. Like someone had a steak on a barbecue. I covered my mouth as the thought brought my bile rising again. I had to get away.

Shakily I got to my feet and made my way to the opposite side of the wreckage again. I didn't know what to do with Jerry's body. I had no shovel and no way to bury him, but I knew I could not be near him right now. The smell, the sight. I felt bad for my repulsion, but in this situation, I knew I had to look out for myself. I had to get help, had to get home.

Stumbling slightly, I stopped next to the wreckage and attempted to pry the door open. The metal was still warm but not enough to burn my hands. I pulled my hoodie sleeves down over my hands to shield my palms from the heated metal. After a few attempts, the door opened slightly with a groan and I got my first real look at what was left of the interior.

The storage totes, once holding food and supplies for the villagers, were nothing more than melted blobs of disfigured rubber and ash. I found my day pack, or what was left of it. It was scorched in spots and a quarter-sized hole was burnt through the nylon pocket. Inside, the contents were unharmed: a bottle of water, two protein bars, an apple, my wallet, cellphone, notebook, and a pen. I grabbed the phone to see if it still worked. The screen was intact but the phone was off. I crossed my fingers and pressed the power button, hoping the heat had not ruined it. A small squeal of excitement escaped my lips as the phone's screen lit up. My good luck ran out when the phone read "no service" and showed no signal bars lit up. I felt a sob of despair building in my chest. I stood there, pivoting in a complete circle, hoping to find a signal but got nothing. Frustrated and exhausted, I quickly looked around for the radio. Maybe the radio still worked! I frantically dug around in the rubble of the cockpit and found the radio. The handset was hanging limply, half melted. I grabbed it and clicked the button. Nothing happened. I kept clicking, hoping that if I did it enough it would somehow make it work. Eventually, I gave up and let it fall back to the floor. I turned dials, I pushed buttons. Nothing. With a sob, I sat down abruptly on the ashen remains of the broken fuselage. I was totally and utterly alone.

When I had been in the air with Jerry, we had talked non-stop for the hour or so we had been flying. He told me embellished stories of run-ins with bears and the time he thought he was going to have to land on a lake without the floats in place properly. My favorite, though, was how his sister Dee had tried to play a prank on him once by moving his plane to a different hangar and saying she'd seen someone fly off with it.

It had been an easy flight, the weather agreeable, the clouds high, with good visibility. I'm not sure what happened. Jerry was laughing at something dumb I had said when all of a sudden the plane jerked and we watched in horror as dark smoke plumed out from the engine as it started to sputter. He started pushing buttons and levers, fiddling with various instruments that were foreign to me. The plane seemed to respond for a second or two and then suddenly we were free-falling, plummeting toward the earth. I remember grabbing the arms of my seat and squeezing my eyes shut, trying not to scream. I could hear Jerry frantically yelling "Mayday! Mayday!" and mumbling something to himself. The radio crackled to life and a disembodied voice filled the cabin, asking for coordinates. I don't remember much after that, just the wail of the wind ripping past us as we descended into the wilderness, the smoke still pouring out of the engine. I knew that I was about to die. Except I didn't die.

Somehow Jerry had managed to land the plane but with the failed engine and the speed of our descent, it was rough. We finally skidded to a halt when the plane plowed into an old birch tree and the front end burst into flames. I jumped out immediately and ran, tripping and falling as I went. After that, I don't remember anything until I awoke to find the remnants of the fuselage smoldering. Poor Jerry. He must have taken longer to jump out and run. Maybe he was injured during the crash and it slowed him down. I had hit my head during the landing but he must have been injured worse.

As I sat in the plane now, looking at what was left, I felt shame. I should have helped him. I shouldn't have run away, but made sure he was out too. Maybe he wouldn't have died then. I felt tears begin to pool in my eyes at the thought. After a few moments, I wiped my nose on my sleeve and looked around again, this time with renewed fervor. Night was coming soon, temperatures would drop further, and I wasn't getting out of there any time soon. I needed to find somewhere to sleep, somewhere warm and safe from the elements.

The fumes that still lingered inside the plane were strong and were not helping my headache. I decided to check the rear part of the plane, hoping to find anything useful. Sliding the melted rubber tubs out of my way, I slowly moved to the tail of the plane. The cargo area wasn't large, but in a pinch, I may be able to sleep there if the fumes dissipated. I found an extra sweatshirt and a backpack that contained melted protein bars, electrolyte packets, a bottle of water, a lighter, a sleeping bag, and an old metal Indiana Jones lunchbox. Curious, I opened the box to find an emergency locator beacon of some kind, meant for signaling for help from the most remote places. I snatched it and quickly shimmied out of the plane. I turned the machine around looking for a way to activate it. I found a button on the side and pressed it. The beacon began emitting a beeping sound and a light on top pulsed in sync. I'd seen beacons like this in movies and hoped that I had done it right, that someone in civilization would pick up the signal and come to my aid.

***

That afternoon, as the sun slid behind some gray clouds, the temperature seemed to drop a little. I worried about it getting too cold as the day progressed so I tried to stay busy, setting up a campsite of sorts. In a survival situation, I knew it was best to stay near the site of the crash, in the event someone came to the rescue. A plane wreck would be easier to see from the air than a single person like me, currently wearing jeans, boots, and a now bloody dark blue hoodie.

I found an area, sheltered from the wind, roughly two hundred yards from the wreckage, and decided to build a shelter of sorts. A dead pine, lying on its side with its roots exposed, would be the base of my new wilderness home. I quickly worked at breaking off limbs and sticks, leaning them against the rough trunk of the tree. Slowly, a triangular-shaped shelter began to emerge. It wasn't much but hopefully, it would keep me warm at night. Pausing from my work long enough to eat a protein bar and sip some water, I decided to attempt to start a fire next. I would need the heat and light tonight. The entire time I worked, I was subconsciously aware of Jerry's body lying on the other side of the fuselage, out of view. I tried not to think about it, keeping my mind instead on the task at hand.

Using the lighter from the plane, I finally got a small fire started. I fed the hungry flames as they quickly consumed the branches from the dead pine. I moved around the area, my legs hurting with each step, gathering up as much wood and branches as I could use for the fire. Once the flames were burning nicely, I finally decided to assess my injuries and wash my face. I only had two bottles of water so, very sparingly, I poured some onto the cuff of my hoodie and wiped my face off. Turning on the camera on my cell phone, I noticed a cut on my forehead, near the hairline, roughly an inch long. It had already scabbed over so I left it alone. Except for another cut on my right calf, and some bruises here and there, I appeared to be uninjured. I sighed with relief and then yawned. Suddenly exhausted, I slid into the sleeping bag from the plane and lay down near the fire to rest for a few moments.

***

I must have fallen asleep because when I woke up, the sun was starting to dip behind the horizon and the sky was darkening. To my dismay, the fire was almost out, so I quickly added more wood and blew on the embers. Angry at myself for being so stupid and letting the fire, my only heat source, nearly go out, I stood there watching the flames. The fire crackled and popped as it greedily consumed the fresh wood and brush. It was then that I noticed how quiet it was, how mind-numbingly quiet it was, save for the slight breeze that gently moved the flames to and fro. I felt a great sense of despair. I was so alone and no one knew where I was. Sure, I had flipped the emergency beacon's button on but I couldn't be sure that it was transmitting correctly, or that someone was even listening to it.

Another cool breeze whipped past me and I shivered. Remembering the sweatshirt I had found in the plane, I turned and headed back to the wreckage to retrieve it. I had just reached the door of the plane when I heard something.

Movement somewhere close, and then a grunt. Was Jerry alive after all? I suddenly panicked, worried that I had left him alone in need these past few hours, desperate and fighting for his life. I quickly moved around the plane, the sweatshirt all but forgotten.

The sight in front of me will forever be seared into my memory. There, standing over what was now left of Jerry's broken and burnt body, was the largest grizzly I have ever seen. I froze mid-step, every fiber of my being suddenly petrified with fear. I stifled a scream as I watched the bear tearing at Jerry's thigh. Part of the pilot's femur was already exposed, glinting white in the fading light. I wanted to run, vomit, and scream but I felt paralyzed. I just stood there unmoving. The ripping sounds of flesh being roughly pulled from bones and tendons were almost my undoing.

It was then that the bear seemed to notice me. He stared at me for a moment and then slowly stood up on his hind legs, his big snout sniffing at the air. He was smelling me. I felt a warm, wet sensation run down my leg, and as the ammonia smell rose to my nose, I knew that my bladder was now empty. The grizzly seemed to notice the scent also, as he let out another grunt.

I had been taught as a kid not to run from a bear as that made you prey. We were told to stand your ground and make yourself big. Hopefully, the bear would leave you alone, but if involved in a prolonged attack, you were supposed to fight with all you had. Right then, at that moment, I just wanted to run. Run away as fast as possible, screaming as I went. Instead, I slowly backed away, never taking my eyes off the bear. I didn't look him in the eyes. As with an aggressive dog, staring him down would have been interpreted as a sign of aggression.

The bear let out a guttural sound just then and I paused, not moving a muscle. I watched in horror as his lips pulled back revealing teeth, sharp and yellowed. He was breathing heavily, still sniffing, and still watching. As he paused for a moment, I took another step backward, not sure where I was going, but wanting to be anywhere but here.

He growled again, louder and longer, drool glistening off his teeth. Suddenly he returned to standing on all four paws, his long claws snagging at the tundra under them. He began pacing back and forth, grunting and huffing, never taking his eyes off me. Jerry's remains were all that stood between us. I gulped, my pulse throbbing, my breathing shallow. Was this how I was to die? Not by a plane crash but at the hands of a grizzly, my remains never to be found?

I thought about my parents back home in Anchorage. I thought about my twerpy little brother living in their basement, playing video games all day. I thought about my best friend, Devon. I would never see them again.

The large beast started pawing at the ground in front of him, agitated and threatened. I remained still, then slowly raised my hands defensively, trying to make myself look as large as possible. The bear continued to pace, ears forward, watching me. Would he charge? Would it be a bluff or would he be ready to fight? I had nothing on my person in which to defend myself.

I was standing there, arms up, wracking my brain for an idea of how to alleviate this situation. To remove myself completely so that neither of us got hurt. Suddenly, the animal pinned his ears back, and with a loud growl, he lowered his head and ran straight towards me. With barely a second to react, the wretched beast collided with me, pushing me down into the cushioned bed of tundra. With a grunt, I instinctively played dead. Rolling into a fetal position, I held my arms over my face. I tried not to cry out as his powerful paws batted and rolled me a few times. I trembled, trying to appear limp, my eyes squeezed shut. Pain tore through my flesh as I was tossed around as though I weighed nothing. As the attack seemed to be winding down, over almost before it started, I remained paralyzed with fear. Snot dripping from my nose, I clamped my mouth shut tight, trying to hold my screams of terror in.

After a few minutes, the bear circled me, clawing at the dirt, and sniffing my hair. He now seemed disinterested. I slowly opened one eye and tried to look around without moving. From my vantage point, all I could see was the sky, dark and somber, and part of the tree that the plane had plowed into. I strained to listen, to hear any signs that the bear was still there. I heard nothing.

After waiting a few moments, I carefully lifted my head to survey the area. At first, I saw nothing but shadows as the moon started to creep out from behind a cloud. With the sun almost gone, the day's light would soon be extinguished. Still listening, and looking, I slowly sat up. I needed to get away from Jerry. I didn't know if the bear would come back to feed but I didn't want to be there if it did.

I got one foot under me and started to stand when suddenly I felt a searing pain in my right shoulder. Teeth, ripping into my flesh, tearing my tendons. I screamed out as I realized the bear had been behind me and now had me locked in his jaws, shaking me like a rag doll. I kicked out at him, trying to make contact, but only kicked air. The teeth pulled me backward toward the ground, a feral growl filling my ears. The bear's jaw held me in an iron grip and I could hear my bones crushing under the intense pressure.

I screamed and yelled, pleading for my life all the while knowing this beast had no intention of granting my wish.

Suddenly, it let my shoulder go, my arm hanging limply to my side. I tried to roll away but as I did, the great behemoth latched onto my ankle and shook me again. The strength the bear exuded was magnificent and I was no match. Knowing that I was about to die, I decided I wasn't going down without a fight. With all the strength and adrenaline I could muster, I kicked at the bear's face with my free foot, slamming my heel repeatedly into his dog-like nose. I screamed and yelled obscenities, swinging my good arm at his drooling face and slugging whatever parts of him I could reach.

He finally let go of my ankle, blood pouring from his flaring nostrils from where I had kicked him. He stood over me, panting. I could feel his breath, hot and fetid, brush my face as my fear changed to anger. I would not die. Not today. I inhaled all the air I could and let out the loudest, most feral scream I had ever made.

"Not today!" I yelled at the grizzly, who had retreated a few steps yet still stood watching me. "Not today you son of a bitch!" I picked up a rock close to my hip and heaved it at the bear, screaming again. The bear gave me another grunt, but then suddenly bolted and retreated, disappearing into the darkness.

I let out a sob, low and mournful. The sobs wracked my body. I took great gulps of air, feeling like I couldn't catch my breath. Snot and tears, blood and dirt all mingled together on my face and I attempted to wipe it away, trying to clear my vision. I needed to make it to the plane. I had to have some protection in case the grizzly came back again.

After trying to calm down for a few moments, I struggled to get up but my left ankle wouldn't hold me. I couldn't move it and was sure that it was broken. I was too afraid to look at it just yet, but even if I did, I wouldn't have been able to see it due to the darkness. Instead, I crawled towards the fuselage, dragging my useless arm and leg with me. The pain was intense but getting to a safer position was imperative. With each slow movement, I crept closer and closer to the plane, the pain jarring and unrelenting.

When I finally touched the cool metal of the Cessna I started to laugh hysterically. I was going mad, the pain and the trauma were too much. I slowly wrenched open the door, its hinges groaning in protest. It took all my remaining strength to pull myself up into the remains of the cockpit and close the door. I laid down, rolled myself into a ball, and cried. I was cold, injured, and alone. Never had I felt such desolation, deserted by humanity.

The cold night wind outside began blowing, causing the airplane to move slightly to and fro. A draft from a broken window sent shivers down my spine as I huddled to stay warm. The sleeping bag was over by the fire, much too far for me to crawl in my condition. Instead, I used the extra sweatshirt, the one I had come to get before the attack, as a blanket to cover me.

I lay there, watching the red light blinking in tune with the low beep emitting from the emergency beacon, and hoped that someone was watching. That somehow I'd be saved.

Eventually, I fell into a restless sleep. Dreams of bears and corpses seemed to dominate my brain. I would try to shift positions, trying to get comfortable, but then the pain would course through me, waking me up again. The night seemed to drag on forever. I would wake up with a start at every sound I heard outside, wondering if the bear had returned. But he didn't.

***

Morning eventually came, the sky gray, the air crisp. I slowly sat up, but as soon as I did, pain raced through me, making me feel nauseous and dizzy. I was so chilled after laying on the cold metal floor of the plane all night. I needed to get another fire started and I wanted the sleeping bag. My stomach growled, reminding me that I hadn't had anything to eat yesterday except a bowl of oatmeal for breakfast at home and the protein bar in the afternoon. Had that been just 24 hours ago? It felt like forever, a lifetime ago.

I carefully reached towards my backpack in the cargo hold and pulled out the bottle of water and another protein bar. Something rolled around in the bottom and I reached back in and found the apple. The sight of it made my mouth water. I was about to wipe it clean on my shirt when I noticed how dirty and bloody my hoodie was. Giving up on cleaning it, I bit into the apple and sighed. It was the best damn thing I'd eaten in a while and I relished every bite.

When I finished eating, I decided I needed to get warm and assess my injuries. I was procrastinating looking for fear of what I'd see. If the pain I felt was any indication of the severity of my wounds, I wanted to put it off as long as possible.

Slowly shifting to remove my belt, I fumbled with the buckle with my good hand. Fortunately for me, I am left-handed, so I was easily able to maneuver the clasp. Looping the belt around my neck, I was able to eventually re-buckle the belt on the largest hole, making a sort of sling for my right arm. I picked up my right hand, now dangling and useless, with my left one and slid it into the makeshift sling. My shoulder screamed in pain, and I was instantly sweating.

Once the pain subsided to a low roar, I carefully and slowly shimmied my way toward the cockpit door and peeked out. There was no sign of the bear, but my mind went crazy, as different scenarios raced through my head. Slowly opening the door, I gingerly stepped down to the ground, taking care not to jostle my arm or shredded ankle too much. Carefully dropping to my knees as I couldn't walk, I slowly began the long trek towards the remnants of the campfire and sleeping bag. My eyes constantly moving, I quickly surveyed my surroundings for any sign of the bear. I caught a glimpse of Jerry's remains out of my peripheral view. I forced myself to check for the bear, to see if it had come back to finish its ghastly meal.

I swallowed hard and looked. The sight before me instantly had me nauseous and regretting my decision. Jerry, what was left of him at least, was now separated into two parts roughly twenty feet from each other. He was barely human looking at this point, just a mess of flesh and bloody bones. I began retching at the sight. This was too much. I wasn't capable of handling this nightmare.

I pivoted away from the awful scene behind me and began the long and arduous trek towards the campsite. With each movement, pain pulsed through my nerves like electricity. My left hand soon became raw from holding up my weight on the frosted tundra, making each movement miserable. I had to make it. I had survived this far, hadn't I? My mouth in a thin line of concentration, I shoved forward, constantly looking around, listening for the bear.

After what felt like hours, I finally made it to the campsite, exhausted and spent. I pulled the sleeping bag, damp from frost, over me and sat, shivering and delirious. I knew the plane was only 200 yards or so behind me, maybe more, but it felt like I had just run a marathon. I sat there, catching my breath, my eyelids getting heavy.

I eventually fell into a fitful sleep, leaning against the dead pine tree, the sleeping bag cocooned around me for warmth. When I woke up, I felt confused and disoriented. What had awoken me? Was the bear back? I tried sitting up to look around but struggled.

Suddenly, through the mid-morning mist, I heard something. Something quiet in the distance yet getting closer, a small tinny whisper of sound breaking the morning silence. I strained my ears, trying to listen. What was that? The sound was getting louder, more distinct. It was familiar to me somehow but I couldn't place it. And then it hit me–jingle bells at Christmas. Thoroughly confused, I continued straining to discern the source of the sound.

The sound was much closer now, a distinct bell, jingling closer and closer.

Suddenly, I saw it. A dog! A black Labrador came running towards me wearing a red vest and a small metal bear bell attached to its collar. Was this a search dog looking for me? My savior on four feet? I started crying, reaching for the dog, as it bounded over to me. With an excited lick on my cheek, it turned again and was gone, disappearing into the bushes.

"Come back!" I yelled as loud as I could. "Help! Please come back!" I pleaded desperately, my voice hoarse and weak. I tried getting up, but my leg wouldn't hold my weight. I sobbed, broken and delirious. Had I dreamt about the dog? Was this the end for me? I wept uncontrollably when suddenly, between sobs, I heard the bell again. The dog was back! I looked up with my swollen, red eyes and saw a woman running towards me. I reached out to her and the dog, confused and disoriented. Was this real or just a mirage made by my overtaxed brain?

The dog reached me before the woman did, dancing and whining excitedly. I reached out to pet the dog, feeling the soft black fur run through my fingers. The dog was real. It licked at my face while wagging its tail exuberantly.

"Good find, Rowan," the woman praised the dog, as she knelt in front of me. "Are you Kate?" she asked, looking at me and assessing my face and body, for injuries.

When I nodded, the woman pressed a button on the radio clipped to her left shoulder.

"Dog 13 to base," she spoke into it.

The radio crackled to life. "This is base. Go ahead Dog 13."

"Subject found alive, medic requested, over." When prompted, the woman reported our coordinates, and then handed me a bottle of water she had pulled from her backpack.

"Copy. Medic en route." came the static-filled response. I sobbed, relief pouring through me. I took a long sip of the water, relishing the coolness of it as it soothed my parched throat.

"Thank you," I cried, trying to calm my nerves. The dog, Rowan, came and nudged my hand, looking for more attention. I smiled at that, giving her a good pat.

One animal almost took me out, but another one saved me.

AUTHOR'S NOTE

Some of you know that I lived in Alaska for over seven years. While there, I was a part of an amazing canine search and rescue (SAR) group. Rowan, my black Labrador was almost a year old when I joined their ranks and began training. Together, Rowan and I trained to do wilderness searches. We even did some training for avalanche rescue! She and I would practice as a group every weekend, and then in smaller meet-ups throughout the week. SAR is a time-consuming venture but the bond formed with your dog and team is amazing. As such, I have purposely put Rowan in *The Alaskan Terror as* Dog 13 (our old team number) and she is the SAR dog that rescues Kate from the bear. If you've read my other book, *River of Lies*, Dog 13 is referred to again. Also in *River of Lies,* SAR member Kathy and her dog Tara are both based on real SAR friends. So is Dugg, the Golden Retriever. Even Otter, Detective Tess Dane's dog in my crime thriller series, is modeled after Rowan.

Unfortunately, I lost my sweet Rowan to B-cell Canine Lymphoma in February 2020. She was only seven. We did chemotherapy and at first, she seemed to respond to it but a little over a month later, she came out of remission. I miss her terribly and so I add her to my stories so that she will never be forgotten.

ABOUT THE AUTHOR

A.L. Hatcher holds bachelor's degrees in both forensic investigation and forensic pathology as well as an associate's degree in veterinary technology. Because of her love of animals, she was a registered veterinary technician for over 23 years but her true passion has always been writing.

Today, she spends her time caring for her child, reading, listening to true crime podcasts, and writing fiction about crime, suspense, and all things dark. She lives in the Midwest with her family, some chickens, and a couple of rambunctious dogs.

WE'D LOVE TO HEAR FROM YOU!

If you enjoyed this book, please consider leaving a review on Amazon, Goodreads, or wherever you review books. Reviews help other readers find books that may interest them and also help provide author feedback.

Please feel free to follow the author on Facebook, Instagram, Threads, and TikTok @alhatcherauthor or sign up for her newsletter at http://www.alhatcherauthor.com
Email: alhatcherauthor@gmail.com

www.ingramcontent.com/pod-product-compliance
Lightning Source LLC
Chambersburg PA
CBHW022020240626
47154CB00007B/2191